WINDS OF CHANGE

WINDS OF CHANGE

Gwen Hoskins

First published in 2024

Typesetting, design and publishing by UK Book Publishing
ukbookpublishing.com

ISBN: 978-1-916572-96-6

CONTENTS

CHAPTER 1 1

CHAPTER 2 13

CHAPTER 3 24

CHAPTER 4 35

CHAPTER 5 46

CHAPTER 6 56

CHAPTER 7 67

CHAPTER 8 78

CHAPTER 9 89

CHAPTER 10 100

CHAPTER 11 111

CHAPTER 12 121

CHAPTER 13 132

CHAPTER 14 143

CHAPTER 15 153

CHAPTER 16 164

CHAPTER 17 175

CHAPTER 18 185

CHAPTER 19 196

CHAPTER 20 207

EPILOGUE 219

CHAPTER 1

Mel was angry. The anger had been building up inside her all through the long ten hours she'd endured, bumping along in this stuffy, crowded coach. Even the frequent stops to change horses hadn't eased the turmoil inside her. The problem was, she now had too much chance to think, too much time to remember those catastrophic, life-changing events prior to the journey. A month earlier, her life had been comfortable and safe. How could her father have done this? She'd always believed he cared deeply for her. She wanted to scream and shout in frustration but that was not an option. Biting hard down on her lower lip, she managed to get her emotions under control. She didn't want her fellow passengers throwing her off the coach.

As the coach lurched into yet another large pothole, the morose-looking man with large red ears and mutton-chop whiskers woke with a grunt and a belch, adding the aroma of garlic and stale ale to the already stifling air.

'What? What? Are we there, eh?'

The thin lady in a severe, beige-brown outfit sitting next to him quickly turned away and stuck her nose in the air.

'Won't be long now, sir.' The plump, homely lady next to Melody told him. 'I always know Gloucester is close when I see May Hill,' she said to Mel, pointing out of the window to a conical hill with a clump of trees on top. 'Oh, I'm so longing to see my new grandson. Just two weeks old he'll be, you know.'

The lady had talked non-stop ever since joining the coach at the last posting inn. She didn't seem to expect an answer, for which Mel had been grateful. But now her words served to jolt her out of the past and start her worrying about the future. What would be waiting for her at Gloucester – or who?! Would they welcome her – or would they resent a stranger being thrust into their midst? There had been no answer to her letter by the time she'd left Birmingham. Had they even received it?

The lumbering coach drew to a halt in the bustling yard of Gloucester's Bell Inn; doors were thrown open, steps let down, and the weary passengers began to make their way towards the inn. Thankful to be on solid ground again, Melody smoothed her hands over the rumpled skirts of her fashionable black twill travelling outfit, readjusted her leghorn hat that had become dislodged with the motion of the coach, and looked around. The yard was crowded with various vehicles, horses being hitched or unhitched to them. Ostlers and potboys were milling around, shouting orders that mostly went unheeded. Where was her escort for the last stage of her journey? No one seemed to be looking for her. She chewed anxiously at her lower lip. What should she do now? The shouts and smells of the busy yard were overwhelming after the close confines of the coach. One of the many horses being moved around the yard came close to trampling her.

'You'd best move, luv, if you don't want to get yourself hurt," one of the grooms shouted at her.

Deciding it was better to wait in the relative safety of the inn, she retrieved her carpetbag among the pile of luggage offloaded from the coach and picked her way across the puddles and piles of horse dung towards the entrance. But just as she reached it, three rough-looking men staggered out. They were very drunk, and cannoned into Melody, knocking her to the ground.

'Watch it, you clumsy lout.' One told his mates. 'Here, let me give you a hand, Ma'am.' Then, swaying precariously, he tried to bend down to help her. Instead, he was in danger of actually falling on top of her. Melody shrieked and managed to roll out of the way as he hit the ground beside her. The smell of their unwashed bodies made her feel sick.

'What's going on here?' A gentleman who'd been watching his groom hitch a horse to a gig noticed her plight and hurried over. The giggling pair was by then trying to lift their mate upright. 'Come on, you lot,' he shouted to them. 'Get away from the lady or I'll call the authorities. Are you alright, miss? If you give me your hand, I'll help you up.'

Melody stared at the pair of shiny black, brown-topped hessians in front of her nose and decided to trust this hand that was being offered to her. The hand was reassuringly strong and warm, and it somehow felt right. But when she stood up and looked at his face she realised she was wrong. The face in front of her was arrogantly handsome, his jaw square and uncompromising, and his eyes were blue chips of ice. Why should he look at her like that? She had expected friendliness, even indifference; however, this seemed to border on hatred. Gasping in shock, she looked down at her crumpled, muddied, travelling dress. Well, what else did she expect? The flirtatious banter she'd been used to receiving from gentlemen was now a thing of the past, and she would just have to get used to it.

‘Th-thank you,’ she stammered.

“You must be careful. Those men were navvies from the canal digging. We’ve had a lot of trouble around here since they arrived.” He glared at their departing backs. Perhaps his black looks were directed towards the men. Melody hoped so.

‘Oh, you poor thing, are you hurt?’ A young lady in a charming rose-coloured travelling dress rushed up and put her arms around her. ‘Good job you were on hand, Josh. Come on into the inn and have a cup of chocolate. I always find that helps when one has had a shock, don’t you? I’m Fleur, by the way, Fleur Benchard, and this is my brother Josh. Have you just come off the stagecoach?’ Melody found herself shepherded into a private parlour and Fleur was ordering hot chocolates for both of them. It was so comforting to find a friendly face, and she longed to stay near her, but she remembered her manners. The innkeeper hurried over to them.

‘I saw what happened. I’m so sorry, miss. No lasting damage, I hope.’

“No, I’m alright now, thank you.’ She reassured him.

‘It’s them wretched navvies,’ he went on. ‘We’ve had nothing but trouble since they started building that there canal.’

‘But it’s brought you extra trade,’ Josh said, nodding towards the laughter in the public bar.

‘Trade I’d willing do without. It doesn’t give a good impression to decent folk stepping off the coaches.’

‘But it’s bound to bring advantages when it’s finished.’ Mel couldn’t help adding.

‘That’s as maybe, but how many years will that be? In the meantime, we have to suffer this disruption. Though thankfully, the worst of them tend to stick to the waterside taverns. It’s not safe for decent folk to venture around there after dark. I’ll be right there, sir,' he added, scurrying away to serve another customer who was banging his empty tankard on the bar.

Mel turned to her rescuers.

'Thank you again, but I'm fine now. I don't want to hinder you. I'm sure you must be eager to be off somewhere.'

'What about you? Is someone meeting you?' Fleur asked.

'My Aunt and Uncle. I'm sure they will be here soon.' Mel hoped that would be the case. What if they hadn't received her letter? Melody chewed her lip with worry. She wasn't sure how many of her precious hoard of coins it would cost to hire a carriage. 'They live in Sedgwick but I'm not even sure how far that is.'

'Sedgwick – but that's where we live.' Fleur turned excitedly to her brother. 'We could take her with us, couldn't we, Josh?'

Josh frowned. 'Maybe your aunt is late and will be here very soon. Who are you visiting there, Miss – er?'

'Meredith – Melody Meredith."

'Meredith – I don't know anyone of that name in the village,' he continued.

'My aunt's married name is Preston.' Melody explained. 'Her husband is a farmer.'

'We know Hannah and John Preston. They farm Thistlewood. That's just across the fields from Sedgwick Manor — that's where we live. So if no one comes for you, you can come with us. Can't she, Josh?' Fleur said excitedly. Josh stared at his sister and then nodded.

'I'll just go and see if the gig's been fixed then,' Josh said, heading for the door.

'I've been staying with my aunt in Bath, and Josh fetched me home. But the wheel on the gig became loose, which is why we stopped in here,' Fleur explained. She giggled. 'Just as well we did, wasn't it, or Josh wouldn't have been around to rescue you.'

Melody felt embarrassed. 'I'm very grateful and I'm sorry to cause you trouble.'

'Don't be silly. I'm glad I've met you. I've got a feeling we're going to be friends. There aren't many young ladies in our village—only Ruth, the vicar's daughter. She's going steady with your cousin Ben, Hannah's son,' Fleur confided.

Melody sighed. Would Fleur want to be friends with her when she discovered her history, she wondered. Would Josh or their parents even allow it? Josh put his head around the door.

'If you two are ready, let's be away.'

In no time at all the three of them were bowling down Southgate Street, and out of the city. But as they reached the countryside, Fleur's shriek made them all jump.

'Oh Josh, stop.' She pointed across the fields. 'What's happened over there?'

It was a shock to see a great gash across the fields; a huge bare brown crater that stretched as far as the eye could see. Men swarmed over the sloping surface like ants, digging and shovelling, eating into the virgin pastureland, pushing the terrible blemish ever onward.

'That, my dear sister, is the new canal that they are building so that ships can get to Gloucester, avoiding the most treacherous part of the Severn,' Josh explained.

'But it's sacrilege. I've always loved the view from here, and now it's all ruined. It's so ugly,' Fleur almost wept.

'I know, it's a scar, like some vicious sword wound across a lovely lady's face, desecrating this lovely rural scene.' Melody could hear the hatred and bitterness in Josh's voice. She was surprised.

'But it's only temporary,' she pointed out. 'When it's finished it will look just as green and peaceful again. Around Birmingham, where I come from, there are plenty of canals. We don't think of them as scars.'

'No doubt if you were in trade you would welcome them, Miss Meredith, but we don't. Even when it's finished it will bring a lot of boats travelling up and down it. Where is the peace in that?'

Melody was disappointed to hear the disdain in Josh's voice. He was obviously one of the old-time gentry who despised everyone in trade, even now, as the eighteenth century was drawing to a close. Didn't he realise the world was changing? People in 'trade' were becoming the new gentry.

'And it's so big. That hole is enormous,' Fleur continued, almost in tears.

'That's because it's going to be the widest and deepest canal in England. The idea is for the big ships that have up until now not been able to navigate the river Severn, will then be able to sail right up to Gloucester.'

'But surely that must be a good thing,' Mel insisted.

'If it ever gets finished! At the minute it's plagued with accidents and disruptions. The villages along the route not only have to put up with the loss of their farmland, but pillaging and worse from the hundreds of navvies. Even your relatives have lost land, Miss Meredith. Their farm stretches right to the canal edge. Not only that, the money seems to be running out. The shareholders are being asked to contribute even more.'

'But that shouldn't affect us, surely?' Fleur said. Josh shook his head.

'I'm afraid it does, Fleur. Father has invested heavily in this venture.'

'Oh no, is that why I've been dragged back from Bath? And what of my promised 'come out' in London next year? Oh, don't say that is to be cancelled,' Fleur wailed.

'Oh, don't take on so, Fleur. Things may be different by next year. We shall just have to wait and see. Now we must get on.' Josh shook the reins and the gig continued. The view of the canal was temporarily lost from their sight, but it remained firmly in all their minds. How would this canal affect them?

As they continued their journey, nobody spoke, each immersed in their thoughts of the canal and the changes it was bound to bring to the area. Suddenly, Melody became aware of how quiet it was, the only sounds being the muted hooves of the horses on the hardpack earth road, the jingle of the harness, and birdsong. So used as she was to being always amongst crowds of carts, carriages, and the constant shouting of drivers and street vendors, this silence was unnerving, the wide open spaces scary. Everything here was so different from her old life. Would she ever get used to it? She was glad when Fleur broke the silence and started chatting about her time in Bath. She soon had Mel laughing at her impersonations of some of the characters she had met there. They chatted happily for the rest of the journey.

'I hope you like our part of the country, and we can be friends, Miss Meredith. Oh, that's such a mouthful. Can I call you by your first name?' Fleur asked.

'That's not polite, Fleur.' Her brother reprimanded her. 'I think you should apologise.'

Melody laughed. 'Oh, that's alright. Friends call me Mel, short for Melody, so I'd be pleased if you would do the same.'

'That sounds much easier. So Mel it will be. It must seem strange to you if you've always lived in Birmingham.'

'It is very strange. I've never seen so much empty space

before. I confess I find it rather bewildering,' Mel said. Fleur laughed.

'It's not empty. It's full of trees and fields and animals and . . . well . . . things. I'd have thought being always surrounded by houses and people to be scarier.'

'It's whatever you're used to, Fleur. Everything new can be scary at first,' Josh said.

Mel was surprised that Josh could be so understanding. She didn't think anything would scare him. They were now beginning to pass one or two houses at the edge of the road.

'This is Sedgwick. It's only a small village,' Fleur explained. 'Thistlewood Farm is on the other side, as is our house.'

Mel anxiously nibbled her lip. The nearer they got to the farm, the more nervous she became. What if she didn't like them? What if they didn't like her? What if they refused to take her in? Where would she go? She felt as though she was going to be sick. She was about to ask Josh to stop the gig so that she could alight when he slowed the horses and pointed with his whip.

'There it is, Mel—that stone house. That's Thistlewood Farm.'

Mel stared at the long, rambling stone house with its stone-slated roof that dipped and rose in an apparent haphazard fashion, sitting in a puddle of sunshine that was reflected in the mullioned windows. Various other smaller stone buildings were clustered around it. It looked friendly, but appearances could be deceptive. To one side ran a narrow garden filled with neat rows of unidentified plants. To the front was a cobbled yard in which chickens scratched and, as they stopped, several large white birds rushed up to the gate, with outstretched necks and wings, making a terrible quacking and squawking noise. Mel shrank back in her seat in fright. A black and white dog burst out of one of the sheds, barking loudly at them. Although he had frightened the birds away, this new terror seemed equally formidable. How was she ever going to get past it to the house door? But then a man appeared from the shed and shouted at the dog, which promptly stopped barking and lay down, though still keeping a watchful eye on the occupants of the gig.

'Hello there, Josh,' he said. 'What can I do for you?'

'I've brought your visitor, John. We found her at The Bell in Gloucester, where she'd just alighted from the Birmingham coach, and as we were passing your place we offered her a lift.'

Mel looked with interest at the man, who was obviously her aunt's husband. He was a large, stocky man with a bulbous nose and the weather-beaten face of someone who had spent his life outdoors.

'Thank you and, er – welcome miss.'

Mel chewed her lip anxiously. The farmer wasn't expecting her and didn't even know who she was. He couldn't have received her letter. Not a promising start. But she stiffened her back and taking a deep breath, replied.

'Good afternoon, Mr. Preston. I am Melody Meredith.' Seeing the blank look on his face she hurriedly explained. 'My mother was your wife's sister?'

'Oh, yes, from Birmingham. Come on in. Hannah will be pleased to see you. Don't mind old Sam, he won't hurt you, and he'll keep them geese at bay too,' he added, seeing Mel's hesitation. 'Will you both come in for a jar, Josh?'

'Not today, thanks, John. I'd best get Fleur home. I've just collected her from her aunt's in Bath. See you again. Good day, Miss Meredith.'

'Bye, Mel,' Fleur called as the gig moved away. 'I'll be in touch.' Mel gazed wistfully after her and hoped she would, for she felt Fleur was someone she would like to call her friend. Though she did find Josh rather forbidding.

'Come along, lass. Let's be getting you indoors. I've got more stock to feed before supper time.' John took up her bag and walked to the farmhouse door. Mel followed, whilst keeping a sharp eye on the geese, now at the other end of the yard but still cackling loudly.

She was ushered into a large warm kitchen full of appetising smells, reminding Mel that it was a long time ago since she'd managed to snatch a roll and some cheese at one of the coach stops. They were never allowed long at the stops before the coach would be off again.

'We have a visitor, Hannah,' John said.

The woman bending over the cooking pot turned around and smiled.

'Aunt Hannah? I'm Melody Meredith. I believe that my mother was your sister,' Mel said, shyly.

'Little Melody – is it really you?' Hannah exclaimed, hastily wiping her hands on the large white apron that she wore around her waist. 'The last time I saw you was as a babe in the arms of your poor mother. Come here and give us a hug.' Her Aunt, a plump little lady with twinkling eyes set in a broad, good-humoured face stippled with a multitude of freckles, enveloped Mel in arms that smelled of apples and spices. 'I was so sorry to hear of your mum's death. But that was years ago. I understood your father was bringing you up himself. So what brings you here now?

'Oh, he did. He was wonderful. He taught me all I know.' Mel felt the tears welling up. She swallowed hard and forced herself to speak calmly. 'But . . . But he's . . . He's dead.'

'Oh, you poor dear. Come and sit down and let me make you a hot drink. Have you come all the way from Birmingham on your own, Melody?' Hannah asked, bustling round as she prepared Mel's drink.

She nodded as John continued.

'Well, you're here now and welcome to stay. Isn't she, Hannah?'

'Of course you are, love. Though I'm afraid you'll have to sleep in the attic room as we have a lodger who has the guest room. But you're more than welcome to that.'

'Thank you, Aunt Hannah. That will be fine. I'm so sorry to just turn up like this. It's rather an imposition. I did send a letter but it doesn't appear to have arrived. I wouldn't blame you if you didn't want me.'

'As if I'd turn me own sister's girl away. Beggar the thought. We're pleased to see you. I'm just sorry it's in such sad circumstances, my dear. Here, you just sit there and drink this while I get the supper on the table. John, can you take Melody's bag upstairs?

'That's alright, Aunt Hannah, I'm just grateful you can put me up.' She took the proffered cup and relaxed, finding comfort in the warming liquid. It was a luxury to be sitting on a chair that wasn't shaking and rolling about all the time. She thought back over the last few days and gave a sigh of relief. She had survived so far, and with some determination, she shouldn't have many problems from now on.

It was just as well Mel couldn't see into the future.

CHAPTER 2

At supper, Mel met the rest of the household. As well as her aunt and uncle, there was her cousin, Ben, a strong lad with an open, honest face and a shock of mousey brown hair, and their lodger, Rupert Johnson, who was the canal's resident engineer. Mel wasn't sure what to make of him. He was certainly handsome and had a charming smile. But still, Mel felt wary of him, though she couldn't say why. It was obvious that there was no love lost between Ben and the engineer. Ben, as her Aunt Hannah explained later, worked the farm with his father, and resented losing some of their land to the canal company. But John felt that the rent Rupert Johnson paid helped compensate them.

'So who's looking after your father's business now?' John asked during the meal.

'No-one. It's – it's gone.' Mel blinked hard to try and prevent the tears.

Hannah looked up startled.

"Gone?' She repeated. 'I don't understand. I thought he was a successful cotton merchant.'

'He was, but then he had a run of misfortune. He'd

recently bought his own ship for importing the cotton, which meant he had to borrow money. But the ship was lost on its first voyage. Then there was a terrible fire at the main warehouse and the remainder of his stock was lost. He just walked into the burning warehouse. They say he must have thought someone was still in there. But he never came out again. The house and contents went to pay his debts. Now I've nothing, I was hoping I could live with you.'

'We can't afford another mouth to feed,' Ben said callously. 'We're struggling ourselves now the canal has taken half our land.'

'Ben!' Shocked, his mother reprimanded him.

'I'd work for my keep, and I don't eat much,' Mel told them desperately. Where would she go if her aunt and uncle didn't want her?

'What sort of work do you think you can do in those fancy clothes?' Ben continued, nodding towards Mel's fashionable travelling gown that she was still wearing. 'A farm ain't no place for any empty-headed city miss. We don't have time for no tea parties and shopping trips.'

'I'm not empty-headed,' Mel said defiantly. 'I used to do all Pa's bookwork for him at the factory.'

'Maybe Mr. Johnson can employ you to help with the canal books,' Ben suggested, with a sneer. Rupert, who hadn't spoken at all throughout the meal, looked up, startled.

'Oh no,' he said quickly. 'Certainly not. That would be very unethical. No one but me is allowed to touch these books. Any mistake in them and I could lose my job.' For a split second, Mel saw pure hate in his eyes as he looked at her. But then it was gone, replaced by a bland smile. She told herself she must have been mistaken.

'Stop it, all of you. Melody is my niece and she is grieving.

So, for now at least, she is staying with us. We can think about the long-term later on,' her aunt told them firmly.

Mel thanked her aunt. But soon as supper was over, she pleaded tiredness and, taking the proffered candle from her aunt, wished them all goodnight and escaped up to her room, before the threatened tears overwhelmed her.

As she dropped the door-latch, Mel held the candle up high and looked around the sparsely furnished room, with its bare wooden floorboards and sloping, beamed ceiling. The candlelight cast flickering shadows over the uneven, whitewashed walls. She sighed. So this was where she'd be sleeping from now on. A far cry from her old room. But she knew she should be grateful. At least her aunt had tried to cheer the place up with a colourful patchwork quilt on the narrow bed and a freshly pegged rag rug on the wooden floorboards beside it. She'd even left a pewter jug of warm water beside the bowl on the washstand so that Mel wouldn't have to wash with the others, downstairs in the scullery. Shivering with cold, she hung her twill carriage gown and other clothes over the back of the wooden, ladder-backed chair next to her carpetbag, and slipped on her long flannel nightgown. After rinsing her hands and face, she blew out the candle and climbed quickly into bed.

But the bed was hard and sleep was elusive. Mel lay there staring at the moon through the curtainless window. A luminous half-moon with ribbons of grey cloud scudding over it like wisps of smoke. No, she mustn't think of smoke. She screwed her eyes up tight. When she opened them again, heavier, darker clouds were rapidly moving in. Soon they had blotted out the moon completely, leaving only a deep blackness; as black as her own unknown future. Then the tapping began, spasmodic at first, building up to an insistent staccato. Was it the sound of dead souls, clambering to come in? Mel gripped the edge of the bedclothes, trying to convince herself it was only the wind in the trees.

A bright flash made her jump, followed by a terrifyingly loud crash of thunder. Mel curled up in a small ball beneath the blankets, shaking with fright. Then the rain came; insistent, heavy, drumming against the glass. The wind increased its fury, rattling the very tiles on the roof of the farmhouse, and howling around the chimneys. Rafters creaked and groaned under the strain. Storms had never sounded like this in the city. Mel was terrified, convinced that the old house was about to fall apart around her ears. How she wished she was back in her familiar half-tester bed with its soft goose feather mattress that she could snuggle down in and feel safe. Would she ever feel safe again? Turning her face into the pillow, she finally gave way to the tears that she had kept at bay all day. Tears for fear of the storm, tears for her father and all that she had lost, and tears for not knowing what the future would hold. Or how she would cope in this strange new world, where nothing was familiar. Eventually, she cried herself to sleep.

The next morning, Mel woke with a start, staring up at the beamed ceiling. She couldn't hear a thing. She panicked, wondering where she was. The storm had blown itself out and the silence was unnerving. Then it all came back to her and homesickness overwhelmed her, making her feel physically sick. What was to be her role in this unfamiliar world? She had no knowledge whatsoever of the countryside. Always having found security amongst the rows of houses and warehouses, she longed to hear the reassuring click of horses' hooves and the rattle of cartwheels on cobbled streets outside her window. Even the cries of the street vendors would have been a comfort. She was now miles from everything that she'd ever known. The shock of the recent events crowded in on her, especially the sudden death of her father

'Why papa?' she cried. 'Why did you do it? Why did you leave me to face all this on my own?'

Her father had always looked for the easy road. In latter years, whenever there was a crisis, he had relied on Mel to steer him through it. She had always been the stronger of the two. But this time she had been unable to find a way. There had been no way. And her father had broken under the pressure. But no one knew how much Mel had helped her father with the business. They'd kept it a secret between the two of them, so as not to undermine his authority. Society would have been aghast had they guessed. Business was considered to be no place for women. However, Mel had relished it. But because no one was aware of this, and with her father gone, she was packed off to live with an aunt she didn't know, to live in the country, an environment so alien to her it was unreal.

However, what was done was done, and she would either have to buckle down and make the best of the situation, or take her father's way out. And she knew she could never do that. Splashing her face and hands with cold water on her washstand, she sorted out her plainest dress from her bag. It was no good putting on fancy clothes if she was going to convince everyone she was prepared to work for her keep. Having been used to the assistance of a personal maid, she found even this frock a bit of a problem. After some deliberation, Mel decided to leave off her corsets and several petticoats. Although this felt terribly daring, it was the best she could do without help. Anyway, surely Aunt Hannah wouldn't be wearing corsets with all the work she had to do around the house.

Downstairs, Mel was relieved to find only her aunt, busy at the kitchen range. Plates and dishes were stacked on the wooden draining board and a cast-iron pot stood beside a pile of vegetables waiting to be prepared for the next meal.

'Ah, there you are, lass. Feeling better this morning, are we? Take a seat and get some of this porridge down you. Do you the world of good, that will. The menfolk have already had theirs and gone about their business.'

'It's good of you to take me in, Aunt Hannah. I know your son, and probably your husband too, think I will be a liability. But I promise I will work for my keep.'

Hannah took one of Mel's hands in her own broad, work-reddened ones, and turned it over.

'These hands aren't used to this sort of housework, love. These are the hands of a lady.'

'No, you're wrong. I'm not one of those useless society ladies. True, I don't know much about housework. The servants wouldn't let me help them. But I took care of all the household accounts. I also helped Papa with the business books. In fact, towards the end, I was practically running the business for him. And I can learn. Papa always said I was a quick learner.' She looked beseechingly at her aunt. Surely they wouldn't turn her out? Where would she go? She had no other relations and her friends had melted away after the collapse of her father's business. Even Sir Lionel, her fiancé, had withdrawn his suit once the extent of their debts became known. Her aunt frowned.

'Isn't it unusual for a girl to work in her father's business? Didn't he want you to attend balls and things?'

'No, after Mama died, Papa lost all interest in socializing. He immersed himself completely in his business. But he was reluctant to leave me with anyone, so started taking me to work with him. In the warehouses, I got bored of just sitting around and soon began asking questions about everything. Sam,

Papa's assistant, took pity on me, not only answering most of my queries but also teaching me to read, write and do sums as well. Then, when he saw how much I enjoyed it, he taught me bookkeeping and everything to do with running the company. When he got sick and had to give up work, it seemed only natural for me to step into his place.'

'Well, I never! So you were taught to read and write. So few girls have that opportunity. In that case, maybe you could help me in the stillroom occasionally.'

Mel readily agreed even though she had no idea what a stillroom was. She desperately wanted to be accepted.

'But I am willing to help with the cooking and housework if you'll teach me.' Mel pleaded. 'I really do want to earn my keep, not be a liability.'

Hannah smiled. 'Well, I could do with some help around the house. Sally, from the village, used to help me but she left last week to marry the blacksmith's son.'

'That's settled then. When do I start?'

'If you really mean it, now is as good a time as any. There are the vegetables to prepare for the stew, and today's my day for butter-making.'

* * *

After three days of peeling vegetables, scrubbing floors, and cleaning out fire grates, every bone in Mel's body was aching. She'd never imagined work could be so hard. But Ben's jeering comments about soft city folk made her determined not to give in. Surely, when she was more used to the work, things wouldn't be so bad. As she stretched to ease her painful limbs, she hoped so anyway. Unfortunately, Ben came through the door just at that moment.

'Too much for you, is it?' He taunted. 'Told you this was no place for you. Why don't you go back where you belong?'

'Oh, you'd like that, wouldn't you? But you won't get rid of me that easily, Ben Preston,' Mel retorted. Rather than sending her away, Ben's comments merely strengthened her efforts to prove her worth. Grabbing the scrubbing brush, she tackled the stone-flagged floor with renewed energy. Ben just laughed, but as he passed her his foot caught the bucket, spilling dirty water everywhere.

'Oh dear, how careless of me.' He grinned as he sauntered out again.

Mel mopped up the spilt water with gritted teeth, muttering.

'Just you wait, Ben Preston. I'll get my own back one day.'

She was now determined not to give in to self-pity. True, her life had been easy up to now, despite her unusual upbringing. But, even with her changed circumstances, she would survive. She'd show them all she was no softy. She paused, wondering if her father had really given in to self-pity, and taken the easy way out. No, despite what people were saying, she had to hang on to her belief that he had truly thought there were others in that blaze in need of rescuing. Would she ever know the truth? With a sigh, she resumed her scrubbing. Her aunt came in and gently took the scrubbing brush from Mel's reddened fingers.

'I think you've done enough for one day, dear,' she told her. 'Why don't you go out and get some fresh air?'

'Oh, but I haven't finished, Aunt. I'm sorry, I would have been quicker but I knocked over my bucket.'

Her Aunt shook her head.

'I saw what happened, Mel. Ben shouldn't have done that. He's not really a bad boy. He'll soon get used to you. Now you go and get some fresh air. You've been working very hard. But you really haven't got anything to prove, dear. I know you want to help, but you don't have to kill yourself in the attempt. You can always be certain of a home here for as long as you wish. So don't worry.'

Mel wiped the back of her hand across her eyes. 'Thank you, Aunt Hannah,' she said.

But her aunt was already heading back to the scullery with Mel's bucket. Mel took off the long sacking apron she'd been wearing to protect her dress, and, doing as she was told, went outside.

At last, after the terrible weather of the past few months, the sun was shining and Mel revelled in the feel of its warmth on her face. By now she was getting used to the open spaces of the countryside, and it no longer worried her. She was surprised at how much greener everything had become during the short time since she'd arrived. The trees were showing tight pink buds and the air was full of birdsong. As she walked through the herb garden, her long skirts brushed the thyme and rosemary bushes, wafting up delicious scents. Mel was enchanted. She'd never imagined a world like this. She spun around, laughing out loud.

'You sound happy, Miss Meredith.'

Mel blushed. She hadn't heard Rupert come up behind her.

'How d'you do, Mr Johnson. Who wouldn't be happy on such a beautiful day?' she asked him.

'Yes, well, at least now the weather's dried up, the men can get more digging done,' he replied, nodding towards the canal workings they could see in the distance.

'Is it all going well?' she asked.

'Of course it is.' He looked at her sharply. 'Why shouldn't it be? Although all this rain we've had lately hasn't helped. And don't you go poking your nose into my books either, even if you do fancy yourself as some sort of secretary. Nobody touches my books, is that understood?'

'Yes, Mr Johnson.' Mel sighed. It seemed he was someone else who disliked her. Was she to make any friends in her new world? They were interrupted by Fleur, who came trotting up on a lovely white pony.

'Hello, Mel. Are you settling in alright?' she called.

'Fleur! How lovely to see you again.' Mel patted the pony. Here at least was one person who was prepared to be her friend. 'Yes, I'm getting used to things a bit better now. Oh, do you know Mr. Johnson? He's the canal's resident engineer.'

'No. I haven't had the pleasure, Miss – er . . . He finished uncertainly with a small bow.

'Pleased to meet you, Mr. Johnson. I'm Fleur Benchard, from the big house. Are you the one responsible for that eyesore over there,' she demanded, waving her riding crop in the direction of the canal workings.

'That 'eyesore', as you call it, young lady, will be the broadest and deepest canal in the whole of England. Up to eighty feet wide and eighteen feet deep,' the engineer told her proudly.

'But why is it to be so wide?' Mel asked. 'Up in Birmingham, where I come from, there are lots of canals but they aren't that big. The boats on them are quite narrow."

'This canal will be big enough to take sailing ships right up into Gloucester docks. It means that they won't have to navigate the treacherous water of the River Severn just below Gloucester. It's an engineer's very complicated and skilled job to make sure it all comes together right,' he boasted. 'Of course, when it's finished it won't look like that. We are creating a beautiful, and practical, work of art. You will be able to enjoy many delightful picnics beside it, I promise you,' he added, smiling at Fleur.

Fleur was by now looking at Rupert with wide-eyed admiration. Mel sighed. She didn't know what to make of the engineer. He was a handsome, charming man, but something didn't seem right. Yet despite her reservations, Mel felt herself attracted to him. Was her new friend smitten as well? Just then, her aunt called her in to help with the supper and she reluctantly left the two of them talking about the statistics of canal building. Did Fleur really understand what he was talking about or was she just fascinated by the man himself? Mel hoped it wasn't the latter.

CHAPTER 3

The next day was Aunt Hannah's baking day, so she asked Mel to feed the chickens and collect the eggs. Mel looked at her in dismay. She'd been quite happy to help out in the house but to go amongst the animals—she didn't know if she had the courage. After all, she was a city girl. She'd never had anything to do with animals except the horse that pulled her gig, and even then its grooming was always done by someone else. But she knew if she wanted to be accepted here, she was going to have to do it.

Taking a deep breath, and with a shaky hand, she lifted the latch on the back door. Stepping out into the yard she was faced with her worst nightmare – the gander and his retinue of geese. The gander spread his wings. Flapping and squawking loudly, he thrust out his neck and came rushing at her. She was about to turn tail and run when her uncle called out to her.

'It's alright, lass. Just stand still and look him straight in the eye,' he called. 'Let him know who's boss and then he won't bother you again.'

Mel, her knees shaking, took a deep breath, pressed her back against the wall and stood there, staring at the angry bird.

Thankfully, the gander stopped, his vicious beak only inches from her. She shouted at him to go away and leave her alone. To her relief, his wings settled back, and, fluffing his feathers, he regarded her with tiny bright eyes. Behind him, his wives squawked encouragement from a safe distance. Mel didn't move, just stared back at him. Then, with one last strident screech of disapproval, he turned and, gabbling to his wives, waddled away. Dutifully, the other geese fell into step behind him. Letting out a breath that she hadn't realized she'd been holding, she looked across at her uncle. He came over to her, smiling.

'Well done, lass, that took grit, but you did it. We'll make a country girl of you yet. Come on, I'll show you around the rest of the farm.' With legs that still hadn't stopped trembling, Mel followed her uncle across the yard.

'Aunt Hannah told me to feed the hens. Can you show me where they are, please?' Mel asked as soon as she could speak again without shaking.

'Of course, this way.'

As they passed a low-walled pen, she heard a lot of grunting and squealing.

'Whatever's in there?' she asked nervously. Her uncle chuckled.

'That's our Bertha. Come and see.'

Wondering what on earth a 'Bertha' was, she edged closer. She was confronted by an animal with a large snout and an open mouth that looked as though it would like to eat her. She jumped back.

'That's our prized pig,' he explained, giving it an apple that those strong jaws soon made short work of crushing to a pulp. 'She just had ten little piglets.' He nodded towards the jumble of small, ginger animals that were fighting their way out of the hole at the back of the pen, squealing loudly. All perfect miniatures of their mother. Mel laughed with delight.

'Oh, they're gorgeous. I want to cuddle them.'

Her uncle shook his head. 'I shouldn't try it, lass. Old Bertha would soon have a lump out of your leg. The hens are over there. Take a bucket of grain from in that barn, scatter it on the ground and collect the eggs in the bucket. Do you think you can do that?'

Mel nodded.

Good girl,' he added. 'When you're done I'll introduce you to the cows.' He went off, leaving Mel to cope on her own.

The barn was huge, with big double doors that were open to the yard, and a high vaulted ceiling. Staring up into its lofty dimness, she could just make out what looked like a large white bird with saucer-like eyes perched motionless on one of the beams. Mel shivered. What other strange animals lived on this farm? She quickly found the grain in a stone bin in one corner and, scooping some into the bucket, headed back out into the sunshine.

While the birds were busy pecking at the grain on the ground, Mel ventured into the hen-house and gathered up the brown eggs that nestled in the straw. But there was one hen still sitting on some eggs. Carefully setting the bucket on the floor, she tried to push it off. But it turned and pecked her hard on the hand. She jumped back with a yelp, just as Ben appeared at the door. Startled, she whirled around and knocked over the bucket, breaking several eggs.

'I knew you were useless. Can't even do a simple job like collecting eggs without breaking them.' Ben was standing in the doorway glaring at her.

'I wouldn't have knocked them over if you hadn't crept up

behind me like that,' she retorted, carefully replacing the least damaged eggs into the bucket.

'Well, aren't you going to get the eggs from under that hen, or are you going to stand looking at her all day.'

'You're so full of yourself – you do it.' Mel snapped.

'Fancy being scared of a hen! There's nothing to it. You just slide your hand under her from behind and take the eggs, see.' He handed her two eggs. Mel was surprised by how warm they were. 'Of course they're warm, silly. Now take them indoors, if you can manage it without breaking any more.'

Mel turned away, biting her lip to prevent tears of anger and frustration from welling up. Why didn't he realise she was doing her best?

Her aunt was so understanding about the broken eggs that Mel found herself on the verge of tears again.

'I'm sorry, Aunt Hannah. It isn't like me to keep crying like this. I usually never cry. Papa used to say, keep your chin up, and grin and bear it,' she said, vowing that from now on that's what she'd do.

'You mustn't take what Ben says to heart, love. He's going through a difficult time himself at present, not only because of the canal but also because things don't seem to be going too well between him and his girlfriend, Ruth.'

'And now I'm just one more encumbrance to cope with. I'll try not to be too much of a hindrance to you all.'

Hannah put her arm round Mel's shoulders.

'Don't be silly. You're not a hindrance. You're a great help. And you can be an even bigger help by chopping these onions for me. Then if anyone sees you've been crying you can say it's the onions,' Hannah told her with a chuckle. Mel decided that in future she would try harder to make friends with Ben. After all, she wasn't the only person having to adjust to change.

Her aunt had told her that they were yeoman farmers, which meant John Preston owned Thistlewood farm, unlike most of the farms around here that were rented from the lord of the manor. So seeing part of it disappear into some huge muddy chasm must be heartbreaking for Ben. It would be like seeing part of your inheritance disappearing into that hole.

The following day was Sunday. After the animals had all been attended to, everyone changed into their best clothes and walked across the fields to church. Mel was surprised to see that even Rupert Johnson accompanied them. Mel was glad of the opportunity to wear one of her better dresses again. Although because she was still in mourning for her father it was black, she'd added a lace collar and cuffs to brighten it. Aunt Hannah looked splendid in a purple gown and even her uncle and Ben looked smart in frock coats and breeches of a quiet hue. The engineer however seemed to have dressed for the assembly rooms rather than a village church service., his blue superfine coat contrasting with a red embroidered waistcoat and buttermilk breeches. Who was he hoping to impress, Mel mused?

The church was only across a field, and as the weather was fine, they didn't bother to get out the cart. Instead, they enjoyed the pleasant walk. Sitting in church with the Prestons, Mel took the opportunity to study the other worshippers. Just as the service was about to start, the old oak door creaked open again and Lord and Lady Benchard entered, followed by Josh and Fleur, and took their seats in the front pews. Mel's heart fluttered. She hadn't seen Josh since meeting them at the coaching inn and had forgotten how imposing he looked. Dressed in a dark green cut-away coat, a moss green waistcoat and buff breeches, his understated elegance made Rupert's finery seem tawdry in comparison. As they passed the Preston's pew, Fleur gave Mel a discreet wave. The Rev. Crosley was a dapper, middle-aged gentleman with a pudding face and kind eyes who delivered his sermon with great sincerity. Mel found his words comforting.

Afterwards, he took time to have a few words with everyone as they were leaving. He was introducing Mel to his daughter, Ruth, when Ben came up to them.

'Ruth and I are walking out,' he told her, proudly.

After meeting Ruth, Mel was surprised. There seemed to be an unwavering air of serenity surrounding the girl, whereas Ben oozed raw energy. But then, she mused, they say opposites attract.

'I trust you are settling in well, Miss Meredith?' Josh's voice startled Mel.

She turned round to find him standing close to her. Again she felt that fizz of attraction between them that had been present at the coaching inn. Looking into his eyes she thought she saw a flicker of desire there, but it was quickly masked. Forcing down the sudden surge of happiness his presence aroused, she smiled.

'Very nicely, thank you, Mr. Benchard. I am learning to appreciate the countryside.' But, disappointedly, he was already turning away to speak to her uncle.

Fleur came hurrying up to her. Soon, all thoughts of Josh were forgotten amongst Fleur's enthusiastic chatter. But Mel noticed that all the time they were talking, Fleur's gaze kept straying to where Rupert Johnson was talking to a group of the locals.

'I expect you're missing the distractions of Bath,' Mel said, trying to take her friend's attention away from Rupert. She was really rather worried about Fleur's obvious interest in the engineer, though she still wasn't sure why. It couldn't be jealousy, because, although he was handsome, he came off as a poor second next to Josh. Reluctantly, Fleur turned back to Mel.

'Yes, although it's good to be home. I'm finding it hard to get used to the changes. I always thought our part of the world would stay the same forever. But how about you? I promised to show you around and I haven't yet. Maybe we could get together next week sometime?'

'I should like that. We could. . . .' Mel paused as they became aware of raised voices from the group around the engineer.

Words such as 'missing sheep', 'broken fences' and even 'lost farmhands' reached the ears of the startled onlookers. As the volume increased it was obvious the situation was becoming very heated. Rupert was beginning to look very fraught. Mel noticed Ben looked like he was hoping to join in. Ruth caught his arm and, with a rueful smile, he turned back to her. Josh was helping his mother into their carriage, but when he noticed the fracas he quickly went over. With a few words, he somehow managed to calm the waters.

'What did they mean, "Missing sheep"?' Mel asked her uncle.

'The navvies are suspected of stealing the odd sheep to supplement their diet,' he explained. 'They've got themselves rather a bad name, but they work very hard under difficult, and sometimes dangerous, conditions. They're not really bad but they're far from home, so you can understand them going a bit crazy on the drink when they get paid.'

'But "Lost farmhands"! Surely they don't kill them?' John laughed.

'No, those are the ones who have left the farms in favour of canal building. You see, a lot of farm work is only seasonal and digging canals is continuous.' Mel was surprised at her uncle's reactions.

'I thought you were against the canal, yet you sound sympathetic.'

'Just understanding. It's true, I didn't want the canal here, but it is here and we just have to accept it. You can't stop progress. Unfortunately, Ben doesn't see it like that. I worry about him. He can be a bit hot-headed sometimes. But Ruth is a good influence on him. The sooner they get married the better, in my opinion. Though of course, his mother would rather they wait a bit. But it's nothing for you to worry your pretty head about. I'm glad to see that you and Fleur are getting along. You need to make some friends. It can't be easy for you being pitched into such a different environment.'

'Oh, I'm fine. I'm stronger than I look,' she assured him.

He laughed. 'I reckon you're right. I shouldn't be surprised that you've hidden depths. Now, we'd best be getting back home. Some beasts need feeding.'

With the excitement over, everyone began heading home. Making their way back across the fields, the men walked in front, Ben still arguing with his dad.

'I wish Ben wasn't so worked up about the canal,' her aunt confided in Mel. 'Trouble is, I've heard that Rupert has been making advances towards Ruth. That upsets Ben even more.' Mel shook her head.

'I think Rupert makes advances to all the females, though he doesn't seem to be serious about it.' Hannah sighed.

'That as may be, but doesn't he realise the damage he is doing to other relationships?' Her aunt suddenly looked startled. 'Has he been making advances to you, too?'

Mel laughed. 'Oh no, ever since I threatened to check his

books he's made a point of avoiding me. Makes you wonder what he's trying to hide though.'

'You're a sensible lass – got an old head on young shoulders. Comes from helping your father in his business, I suppose.'

This may have been true, but it didn't stop Mel from yearning for the impossible—a secret she kept strictly to herself. The conversation turned to more general topics for the rest of the journey.

The following day, being Monday, was wash day. As soon as she was up, Mel helped carry buckets of water from the pump in the yard to fill the brick-built copper in the washhouse. A fire was lit in the fire hole underneath it. Then it was indoors to change the beds and collect together the dirty clothes while they waited for the water to heat. Molly Pugh, the carter's wife, always came in to help Hannah with the washing so Mel was given the chance to escape for a couple of hours. She decided to explore in a different direction. Round the corner from the washhouse, Mel discovered a strip of grass that bordered a pond. A beautiful tree lent over it, dangling its graceful fronds in the water. Half a dozen green-headed ducks, wriggling their tails, waddled around the edge and then flopped into the water. On the far side of the pond, the gander paraded up and down, his head held high, pretending not to notice Mel. His geese fluffed their feathers and settled down to rest at the water's edge. Following the footpath through an orchard, she met Ruth. She had set up an easel and was painting the blossoms just breaking out on the fruit trees. She looked quite a picture herself, with her long blonde hair glinting in the sun, and eyes as blue as the sky. Mel sighed, running her fingers through her own unruly auburn curls. If she looked like that then perhaps . . . But she knew it was no use dreaming. They chatted together easily whilst she admired Ruth's skill.

'I'm lucky that Ben's dad allows me to set up my easel anywhere on the farm so I never run out of subjects to paint.'

'Don't you get lonely sitting out here on your own?'

'Oh no, I love doing it. Time slips away unnoticed.' Ruth giggled. 'Sometimes Father gets so cross because I'm late home for meals.'

'Then I'll leave you to it. I'm going to walk a bit further towards the canal.' With a wave, Mel continued on her way.

The day was perfect. Sunny, but with a breeze just strong enough to nudge cotton-wool clouds across the blue sky. Sheep grazed contentedly in the distance. A far cry from Birmingham and her past life. But suddenly she was overwhelmed with homesickness. It was as though a black mist had descended, seeping into her very soul. The memory of losing her father rushed in with a pain so intense that she cried out. Also, the feeling of guilt. He hadn't been in her thoughts for several days. How could she push him away like that? Was she such a bad daughter? She sank to the ground, her long skirts billowing around her. With tears streaming down her cheeks, she buried her head in her hands.

'Are you hurt? Do you need help?' A voice with a soft Irish accent made her look up. Concerned blue eyes looked at her from beneath a shock of black hair.

Mel dragged her sleeve across her eyes. 'N– no, just feeling a bit homesick.'

He gave a cheeky grin, his eyes now sparkling with mischief.

'Ah, I can identify with that, being a long way from home myself.' Judging from his clothes and his rather muddy face, she guessed he must be one of the navvies. But he didn't look very scary. 'Connor O'Flynn at your service, miss. Self-appointed spokesman for the canal workers. You must be the new lass from the farm. I was on my way there to see Rupert Johnson, to report the spate of unexplained breakages to ladders and equipment.'

'Mel Meredith,' she told him. 'But you won't find Mr. Johnson at the farm. I heard him say he was going into Gloucester.'

'Thanks, you've saved me a journey. Here, give me your hand and I'll help you up.'

Suddenly there was a shout, and they looked up to see a man on a big black horse galloping toward them, waving his riding crop in the air. As he got nearer, Mel recognised Josh Benchard.

'Get away from her, you filthy Irish scum,' he was shouting. 'I'll thrash you to an inch of your life.'

CHAPTER 4

'No,' shouted Mel. The word 'scum' burnt into Mel's brain like acid. She remembered watching another 'Gent' shouting that at one of his employees and then beating him to death with his whip. She'd been powerless to intervene then, but not this time. She'd believed Josh was above that sort of thing, and it hurt to discover that he wasn't. Recognising Connor as a navvy, he'd immediately presumed that he was attacking her. But Connor had only been helping her. If he was injured it would be her fault. She had to stop Josh. As the big horse loomed nearer she struggled to stand up. But in her haste, her feet became tangled in her long skirts and she fell forward right into the path of those steel-tipped hooves. With a curse, Josh frantically reined back his mount, which reared up onto its hind legs. Before it could come crashing down again, he managed to pull its head around so that the descending hooves missed her, though only by inches.

'You stupid little fool. Are you trying to get yourself killed?' he shouted.

'If you hadn't come charging in like some puffed-up medieval knight, you would have realised that Connor was helping me, not attacking me.' She yelled back at him, as Connor helped her to her feet. Josh jumped off his horse and, slipping his arm through the reins, walked over to her.

'Oh, so it's 'Connor', is it? Are you so desperate for a man that you had to look for one among that rabble? If I'd known, I'd have offered my services,' he jeered.

'Don't be so disgusting. It seems to me that Connor has more honour than a so-called 'Lord' like you.' But as Mel stared up at Josh, she couldn't help noticing how well his buff jodhpurs fitted over his firmly muscled legs. Quickly, she re-focused her mind on his smug arrogance.

'Look, if you're OK now, Miss Mel,' Connor interrupted, 'I'll leave you two to your lover's tiff and be off.'

'Lover's tiff!' They both round on him in unison.

'We are not lovers, and never will be.' Josh shouted.

'I was under the impression that only a moment ago you were offering your services.' Mel reminded him.

'I didn't mean it.' Josh gritted his teeth.

'Of course not, you wouldn't stoop to associating yourself with 'trade'.

'What on earth are you talking about now?' Josh shook his head in exasperation.

Connor shook his head in disbelief and, having assured himself Mel would be alright, left them to it and made his way back towards the canal.

'Just because my father made an honest living through trade, you think we are below your sort. Let me tell you, I've known 'your sort' bankrupt tradesman just because they don't think it necessary to pay their bills on time. They give no thought to the women and children they force out onto the streets to starve.' There was no stopping Mel now. 'They're so puffed up with their own so-called importance that they never consider others.'

'You shouldn't make accusations about things you know nothing about,' Josh hurled back.

'That's where you're wrong.' Mel lifted her chin and stared Josh straight into his eyes. 'I looked after my father's books for the last few years of his business. I know exactly how some of you so-called superior men held honest businessmen to ransom without a single qualm. And yet if it was a gambling debt, that was considered a debt of honour and had to be paid immediately. You make me sick!' With that, Mel turned on her heel and, with her nose in the air, marched back towards the farmhouse.

Josh shook his head in bemusement, remounted his great horse and continued on his way.

As Mel neared the house, she didn't feel up to facing others in her present state of mind. Although the incident had banished the feelings of homesickness, she was still trembling with anger at the thought of Josh's high-handedness. She hated the thought that he could be so biased that he'd have thrashed Connor without giving him a chance to explain. Did he always ride roughshod over those of lower birth than himself? She wouldn't have believed it if she hadn't witnessed it for herself. He'd seemed such a decent, likeable young man. It just proved how first impressions could be so wrong. She sighed; he was obviously a very complex person.

Skirting round the back of the house, Mel entered the herb garden, sank gratefully onto a seat placed amongst the sweet-smelling herbs, and buried her head in her arms. Why was life so complicated? Only a few weeks ago everything was so cut and dried. She had been content with the pattern of her life, expecting it to continue like that for many years until the time came for her to marry Felix, the man that her father had chosen for her. But then her world collapsed around her. Everything she had trusted in—even Felix—was gone, thrusting her into a life so alien that she was having difficulty adjusting to it. And people like Josh Benchard didn't help. A hand touched her shoulder. She looked up to find her aunt beside her, a worried look on her face.

'Are you alright, my dear?' she asked. 'When you went by the window I thought you looked upset.'

'Oh, Aunt Hannah, I feel so mixed up inside. I don't know what's happening to me. At home, I was always so calm and in control. I never let my emotions get the better of me. I coped with all types of problems while helping Papa with the business and I never once lost my patience. I certainly never cried. Now I seem to be crying all the time. Am I going Mad?'

'Of course you're not, love. It's a normal reaction. You've sustained a terrible shock recently – not only the death of your father, but losing all that was familiar to you, and having to live with strangers.' Her aunt pulled her gently into her arms. 'You're being very brave. But it's bound to take a while to adjust to these changes. It will get easier in time. I know everyone says that and you probably don't believe it at the minute, but I promise you it will.'

'Oh, Aunt Hannah, you're so good to me. It can't be easy for you – having another mouth to feed.'

'Aw, that's no problem. And you've given me something I never thought I'd have again—a daughter. I lost my own little daughter when she was only two, and I was never able to have any more children. So you see, I do know what it's like to lose a loved one.'

Mel rested her head on her aunt's shoulder. 'I'm so sorry. That must have been terrible for you.'

'No worse than losing a father.'

They sat quietly for a while, each with their own thoughts. The late afternoon sunshine enfolded them in its warmth.

A bevy of sparrows squabbled in a nearby bush, while a blackbird combed the ground around their feet, its bright yellow beak searching for insects and worms. A robin flew down and perched on the arm of their seat, its little head on one side as it studied them. Probably hoping they had some food for him. Mel couldn't help smiling at its cheekiness.

'It's good to see a smile on your face again, my dear. But this won't do. I must get a meal on the table before the men come in. You can stay out here if you like.'

'No, I'll come and help you. It will stop me moping,' Mel said with a self-conscious laugh. They made their way back into the house.

The next day Mel was busy helping her aunt clean and peel the parsnips and turnips to add to the pottage pot that was constantly on the hob, when her uncle came in to tell her that Fleur was here to see her.

'Bring her in, John. Don't leave her standing outside,' her aunt said.

'She's brought her horse and she can't bring that indoors,' John replied with a chuckle.

'Oh dear,' Mel sighed. 'I was hoping we'd go for a walk. I can't ride a horse.'

'Don't worry, the horse has a governess cart hitched to it.' John winked at his wife.

'Oh really, John, you shouldn't tease Mel,' Hannah said. Turning to Mel, she added, 'Off you go, dear. A bit of fresh air will do you good.'

'I should take a shawl, the wind's a bit keen today,' her uncle advised.

'Thanks,' Mel called, already on her way upstairs to find her shawl. Upstairs, she paused to look out of the window. She could see Fleur holding the reins of her white pony that was harnessed to a small, four-sided tub-like cart with a little door in the rear. Mel knew she'd feel safe enough in that. How kind her friend was to have thought of it.

But Fleur was not alone out there. Rupert Johnson was with her. They had their heads together and were talking very earnestly about something. Mel frowned. It didn't look as though this was just a casual greeting. What was her friend up to? She hurried downstairs to join them.

'Good morning, Fleur. Good morning Mr Johnson, I'd have thought you would have been busy at work,' she stated rather abruptly.

Rupert frowned. 'I am on my way now. I was just explaining some facts that Fleur expressed an interest in,' he told her. 'But I will now bid you both farewell until another time,' he added, looking straight at her friend.

'I'm surprised you allow that man to be so familiar with you, Fleur,' Mel said once he'd left them.

Fleur looked defiantly at Mel. 'I don't know what you mean,' she said. 'Rupert is a perfect gentleman.'

Mel shook her head. 'Is that the manners of a gentleman – calling you by your given name? And you too, calling him Rupert? I'm not sure your parents, or Josh, would approve.'

'Oh, Mel, don't be so stuffy. We're in the country now, we don't need to stick to town rules here. Besides, Rupert is a very interesting man. I don't know what you've got against him.' Mel wasn't really sure either. There was just something about him that she didn't take to. But what it was, she was at a loss to explain. 'Rupert talks to me as an equal, whereas everyone else around here treats me as a child. I am sixteen and will have my coming-out party next summer. Anyway, enough of that.' Fleur shrugged off her ill humour with a sunny smile. 'Are you coming for a drive with me? I brought the governess cart because I know you don't ride. You really should learn though. Everyone in the country can ride. I'll ask Josh to teach you.'

'Oh no, I'm sure he's much too busy,' Mel hastily pointed out. She didn't think it would be wise to be in such close contact with Josh. He was much too attractive for her peace of mind.

'I'll ask him anyway. He can always say no. But today I thought I'd show you more of the village, as I don't suppose you've had much chance to see it yet.'

'Yes, that would be lovely. I don't seem to have explored much of the area at all.' Mel, glad of the change of subject, clambered in through the little door in the back. With a flick of the reins, they were off, with Fleur pointing out the places of interest. As they passed the church she told Mel that it was built in the 12th century. When Mel expressed her surprise at her knowing this, Fleur laughed.

'No, I haven't been delving into its history. I'm no blue-stocking. It's just that Reverend Crosley is very fond of telling everyone. Apparently, looking up old records is a hobby of his.'

'Well, it's certainly got a fine spire.' Mel observed.

The little pony trotted on, passing the village green, with its stocks in the middle, and an inn sporting a large sign depicting a rather unrealistic picture of a sad-looking cow, though the wording defined it as The Black Bull. Then they passed several small thatched cottages. As they neared the Forge, the Blacksmith came out gesturing wildly with thick, brawny arms at the vicar, who appeared to be trying to calm him.

'Oh goodness, I wonder what that's all about,' said Fleur, pulling the pony to a stop.

'Maybe we shouldn't interfere,' protested Mel, but her friend was already waving to the men.

'Good morning, isn't it a lovely day?' she called.

The blacksmith looked up, growled, and stomped back into his forge.

'I don't think he agrees with you,' Mel giggled, quickly smothering it as the vicar walked up to them.

'Good morning, ladies. You off visiting then?' he asked.

'No, I was just showing Mel the village. But we're turning back now. Can I offer you a lift home, vicar?'

'That's kind of you, my dear. These legs of mine aren't as fit as they used to be.' He climbed gratefully through the little back door of the trap and squeezed his portly frame into the seat next to Mel. 'But could you drop me off at Mrs. Simms' house? The poor old lady is very ill. I don't think she'll be with us much longer.'

'The blacksmith didn't seem too happy,' Fleur prompted.

The vicar shook his head. 'He's worried that his daughter seems to be spending too much time chatting to those navvies. But it's understandable, really. This village has never been over-populated with single men and now, with such a sudden influx, it is very tempting for the girls. Other than locking them up, how can you stop them? I shall be glad when this canal's finished. This used to be such a quiet place.'

'That's just it, the girls have probably found it too quiet,' Mel observed.

'Well, let's just hope we don't get too many long-term problems,' he said shaking his head. Mel wanted to ask him what sort of long-term problems, but he changed the subject to more general topics. However, she was only listening with one ear. She was thinking about the canal, and the effect such a dearth of men must be having on the local villages. Every girl dreamed of getting married and if there weren't many local boys, was it any wonder the girls were looking elsewhere, even if it was forbidden fruit? After they'd dropped the vicar off, Mel asked Fleur.

'Do you find the village too quiet – after the bustle of Bath with all its amusements?'

'It's very different. But I love the countryside here,' Fleur said. 'Well, I did until they ruined it by digging great craters everywhere,' she burst out. 'But Rupert has been convincing me it mightn't be such a bad thing after all,' she continued rather wistfully.

Mel looked at her friend with growing concern.

'Fleur, do your parents know of your friendship with Mr Johnson? Do they approve?'

'Oh, they don't know. There's no reason for them to know, is there? We just talk occasionally, that's all. But Mel, he's so interesting. When he talks of the canals he's built and the places he's been I could listen forever.'

'Oh Fleur, please be careful.' Mel pleaded. 'You should take everything he says with a pinch of salt. I don't believe he's built many canals.'

'You're just jealous, Melody Meredith! Just because he obviously prefers me as I'm prettier than you.' She flicked back her blonde curls in defiance. 'This is all the thanks I get for taking the time to show you the sights. Well, in future you can get yourself around.'

'I'm sorry, Fleur. I spoke out of turn. It's true, I don't really know him. Maybe I'm wrong. I'm just saying, be careful. But I don't want to quarrel. Please forget I said anything. I do want to stay friends.' Fleur was the only friend of her age that she'd made in the district; life would be even lonelier if she deserted her now. 'Anyway, I'm sure you'll forget all about him when you have your coming-out ball. Then you'll have plenty of young men to choose from.'

'It's not as simple as that. A lot of other girls will be competing for their attention. There's no guarantee any of them will be interested in me.'

Mel was surprised at her sudden apparent lack of confidence. 'Don't worry, I'm sure there'll be some handsome duke waiting in the wings, ready to sweep a pretty girl off her feet.'

Fleur laughed. 'Mel Meredith, I do believe there's a romantic heart hidden under that practical exterior. But what about you? Were you due for a coming-out ball?'

Mel shook her head. 'It doesn't work like that with us. We don't go in for balls and things. Business comes first, even in the question of marriage. Papa had selected a suitable man for me. He was a Viscount and although we were only unofficially engaged, there was an understanding that we would be married after two years.'

'That sounds like a horrible way of doing things. Weren't you given a choice?'

'Oh yes, I could have said no and Papa wouldn't have forced me. But Felix seemed a nice enough man, so I was happy to go along with it.'

'So when's the happy day?'

'Never.' Mel sighed. 'After Papa's death, we lost all our money and he cried off. Apparently, he proposed to another lady even before the funeral was over.'

'Seems to me you had a lucky escape.' Fleur put her head to one side and studied her friend. 'So that's why you're so suspicious of men. That's why you don't trust Rupert. But you shouldn't let one experience colour your view of all men. I think Rupert is a good person.'

Mel thought about her friend's comment. Had Felix's betrayal influenced her opinion of Rupert? After all, the only real proof of something suspicious was his reaction to the thought that she might look over his books. But wouldn't any man be resentful of being shown up by a woman? Perhaps she was wrong about the engineer. She wasn't so sure, but she didn't pursue the subject as they'd arrived at Thistlwood Farm.

'Talking of men – isn't that one of the navvies at the back door?' Fleur asked. 'Will you be alright going in?'

Oh, yes, that's only Connor O'Flynn. He's the spokesman for the workers. I expect he's hoping to have a word with Mr Johnson. Thanks for the drive,' Mel said, as she clambered out of the cart.

'I'll be off then. See you sometime.' Fleur flicked the reins and the pony trotted off down the road.

Mel was glad she hadn't noticed that Rupert Johnson was also at the door and that the two men seemed to be having a very heated argument.

CHAPTER 5

As Mel approached, the engineer retreated back inside, slamming the door shut in Connor's face. From the expression on his face, the conversation had obviously not gone well. Mel was curious to know what it was all about. Angrily, Connor whirled round, almost knocking into Mel as she came up to the door.

'Oh, sorry Miss Mel. I didn't hear you behind me.'

'Sounds as though things didn't go as well as you'd hoped?' Mel said, nodding towards the closed door.

'No, that b – err – big-headed engineer doesn't play fair. I come to him with a genuine request from the men and he twists it round and blames the navvies themselves,' he told her bitterly.

'Why, what's happened?'

'A lot of our shovels, wheelbarrows, and such have been sabotaged. I know some of the villagers resent us being here. Why don't they realise that this sort of thing only means we will take longer to finish the job? But instead of offering to find the culprits, the mean old s… Well, he says it must be the navvies themselves and he will deduct the price of replacing them from our wages.' Connor spread his hands in despair. 'I can't understand his attitude at all. It will only make the men resentful, and that does not lend itself to a good working relationship.'

'I'm so sorry. If I hear anything I'll let you know, but I don't really have much to do with the village.'

'Oh no, it's not your problem. You just caught me at the wrong moment. Please don't you worry your pretty little head about it,' Connor told her.

Mel laughed. 'Get away with you and your flattery. It's a waste of time using your Irish charm on me,' she said. Although she was secretly pleased to be called pretty, especially as she didn't consider herself at all pretty, she wasn't about to tell him that.

He gave her a cheeky smile, his anger evaporating in an instant. 'Ah, but you're truly a breath of fresh air, Miss Mel. You take care, mind. And watch out for that Rupert Johnson. I don't know what his game is, but I don't trust him.' Then with a wave, he strode back towards the canal workings.

'You and me both,' Mel mused as she watched his departing back. Then with a shake of her head, she went indoors.

The engineer was in the kitchen, talking to her aunt.

'You want to stay clear of that Irish navvy, young lady,' he said as soon as he saw her. 'He's a troublemaker, that one. You can't trust anything he says.'

Mel was tempted to tell him that Connor had said the same about him, but decided for once it would be prudent to keep her thoughts to herself.

'You can't trust any of them – scum of the earth, they are,' he continued.

Mel looked at him in surprise. That was the second time she'd heard them called that. Was it true or was someone putting the idea into others' heads?

'Surely they are just hard-working men who work under very difficult conditions, Mr Johnson?' she asked him. 'True, there's bound to be one or two bad apples, but I'm certain if you treated them with more understanding and investigated their complaints, you'd realize that.'

The engineer glared at her.

'I've told you before, Miss Mel. Young girls like you know nothing at all about it. So kindly keep your opinions to yourself. If you don't watch it, you'll get yourself into trouble and you'll only have yourself to blame. Now, I'm off up to my room as I have some work to do.'

He left the room, leaving Mel fuming with no chance to reply. She stormed outside to get some fresh air and try and calm down. The gander met her at the back door with his usual aggressive squawking, but she was so keyed up that she just shouted at him.

'Don't you start; I've had enough of stroppy men for one day.'

Much to her surprise, after one final squawk, the bird turned his back on her and, with his beak in the air, strutted off, leading his wives towards the pond. Mel lent on the gate and stared unseeingly at the cows grazing quietly in the field. She couldn't help feeling sympathetic towards the canal workers. Surely they couldn't be as bad as all that! She just wished the locals could look beyond the actual building of the canal and realize the advantages it would bring when finished. Even the countryside, though different, would still have a certain beauty about it. Hadn't she seen it with her own eyes up in Birmingham?

She sighed.

'Instead of mooning around doing nothing, why don't you help me for a change,' Ben said angrily, coming up behind her unnoticed.

Mel whirled around guiltily. 'Of course I'll help, if you tell me what to do.'

'Then come and help me groom the horses. Carter's off sick and I promised to meet Ruth. If I have to do it all myself I won't make it,' he said, already turning towards the stables. Mel followed reluctantly, wondering what new ordeal awaited her. In the stables stood two big black horses. Both had a white blaze down their faces and long shaggy white hair covering their hooves. She had seen them before from a distance, pulling the wagon, but never up close.

'They're giants,' she gasped, nervous to go near them, much less groom them.

'They won't hurt you.' Ben sneered. 'They're gentle giants. Here, take this brush and start on Boxer while I do Captain.'

He handed her a flat oval brush with a leather strap for her to slip over her hand. Gingerly, she began to brush Boxer's side. His skin quivered and she jumped back, dropping the brush.

'Not like that, silly. You're supposed to be grooming him, not tickling him. You have to press hard, like this.' Ben picked up the brush and proceeded to show her. 'D'you think you can manage that?'

Mel nodded, and, taking back the brush, began applying firm smooth strokes as Ben had done. Her confidence grew as she realized that, far from hurting her, Boxer seemed to be relishing it. She began to actually enjoy herself, finding it very therapeutic. Soon, all her antagonistic feelings melted away and she was calm again. They worked in silence for a while until, plucking up enough courage, Mel asked Ben how long he'd been courting Ruth. At first, she thought he was going to ignore her. But then he said:

'Only since last Christmas. It was at the village social. Before that, I'd always thought she was a bit of an insignificant mouse. But that day she was wearing a bright blue dress and it really brought out the colour of her eyes. I remember thinking, "My, she's really pretty!" So I asked her to dance and we just seemed to hit it off together.'

Mel was surprised. She was sure that that was the longest speech she'd heard from Ben.

'So when are you two getting married?' she asked.

Ben shook his head. 'We're in no hurry. We have to wait for a cottage to come empty. I don't think Ruth wants to live in the farmhouse. She says she wants to have her own kitchen.' Mel could understand that. Aunt Hannah had a kind heart, but she'd been running her household for so long that she couldn't imagine her willingly releasing the reins.

'You intend to always stay on the farm then?'

'Of course, this farm has been in the family for generations and it will be mine someday. That is if there's any of it left after that wretched canal has finished eating away at it,' he finished bitterly.

'But when it's completed, it will all look peaceful and green again.'

Ben shook his head. 'But it will never be the same as before. We used to be able to walk from the farm right across the fields to the banks of the River Severn. The canal will be like a barricade fencing us in. Anyway, enough of that—if you've finished, let's go and get something to eat. Um, you've done quite a good job for a city girl,' he told her grudgingly as he examined Mel's handiwork. Mel was elated and felt like skipping back to the house. Maybe she was finally getting to grips with life on the farm. Though what her father would think of her now, she couldn't imagine. With her grubby apron and her auburn hair in wild unruly curls blowing about her face, she was a long way from the sedate office assistant he had expected of her, but she found that she was actually beginning to enjoy this life. Though what of the future? If she was ever expected to go back to that life, would she be able to fit into the many rules and restraints imposed on young ladies in the cities? She rather doubted it.

After their mid-day meal, as Aunt Hannah had said she didn't need her, Mel decided to pay a visit to Ruth at the vicarage. She found her at her easel, painting the profusion of flowers that surrounded her. Seeing her friend arrive, Ruth gladly abandoned her art to fetch a couple of glasses of refreshing lemonade, which she set on a nearby wrought iron table. Then she joined Mel on the swinging garden seat. Mel soon noticed that her friend seemed very quiet and asked her if something was troubling her. Ruth blushed but assured her it was nothing. However, it cropped up in conversation that Ruth thought Mel must be seeing a lot of Ben.

'No more than he has to.' Mel grimaced. 'He thinks I'm a useless city girl that he is obliged to tolerate for his mother's sake,' she said, skating over the truce they seemed to have reached during the grooming of the horses.

'But you must fancy him,' Ruth insisted.

'No way!' She laughed 'Can you imagine me as a farmer's wife? I hardly know the difference between a cow and a sheep.' Ruth, deciding that Mel was no threat to her long-term happiness, relaxed, and Mel was thankful she hadn't lost one of the few friends she'd made since coming to the country. She thought fleetingly of Fleur, whom she hadn't seen lately. Maybe she was just busy with other things. She banished morbid thoughts and the two girls spent the rest of the afternoon in happy girl talk.

Towards the end of the afternoon, the sun disappeared behind the clouds, threatening rain. Mel decided it was time to make her way back to the farm. It was blowing hard by the time she thankfully entered the warm kitchen, where she was greeted by appetizing smells. Her aunt was bent over the old range, already cooking the evening meal.

'Ah Mel, just in time to set the table. Did you have a good afternoon?' her aunt asked.

'Yes thank you, Aunt Hannah. Ruth and I seem to get on well.'

'Ruth's a nice girl. I was pleased when Ben took up with her. I'm sure she'll make him a good, steady wife eventually. Though there's no need for them to rush into things. Marriage lasts a long time. Sounds as though it's getting rough out there. We could be in for a storm,' she said, changing the subject.

Mel remembered that awful storm on her first night at the farm and hoped it wouldn't be so bad. She didn't want to be forced to admit she was afraid of thunder. That would give Ben something else to despise her for, just when she felt she was making some headway. But by the time the men came in, it had started raining hard.

The engineer came in, slamming the door behind him. It was obvious that he was not in the best of moods.

'Damned weather,' he muttered.

Hannah turned on him. 'Mr Johnson, I will not have swearing in my house. Please remember that.'

He scowled. 'Sorry, Mrs P., but this weather's enough to make a saint swear. It will cause havoc down at the diggings. Those wretched navvies are bound to use it as an excuse to down tools again.'

'But surely the rain will make the clay sides dangerously slippery,' Mel couldn't resist pointing out.

'Oh, so you consider yourself an expert in building canals as well now, do you? Well, I'd appreciate it if you kept your opinions to yourself and your nose out of my business, young lady,' he told her ferociously.

'I'm sure she didn't mean any harm, Mr Johnson. Now sit down so that I can serve out the food.' Hannah said, trying to calm things down.

Ben just winked at her when he thought the engineer wasn't looking. Mel lowered her head to hide her smile. Rupert sat down with a scowl and didn't say another word throughout the meal. By the time they'd all retired to bed, the storm had increased in momentum, and Mel once more buried her head under the bedclothes and prayed for morning.

The next morning showed no let-up with the weather. It rained persistently throughout the day. Everyone's mood was as bad as the weather so Hannah suggested she and Mel would spring-clean the bedrooms. Everything was stripped and shaken, floors scrubbed and furniture polished. But they'd finished it all in time to get a quick evening meal of soup that her aunt had left simmering on the range, along with cold bacon, bread and pickles. Nobody complained about the lack of a cooked meal as they were just thankful to sit in the warm kitchen and dry off. Mel, her arms and back aching from the relentless polishing, took herself off to bed early.

Luckily the rain had moved on by morning, though the sky was still a murky grey. As Mel stepped out into the yard she could see merely a glimpse of the sun behind a misty veil of clouds. Water dripped mournfully from the leaves and lay in vast swathes everywhere. In the field, cows stood around, miserably hanging their heads while waiting patiently for milking time. Only the geese stayed stubbornly cheerful, fluffing up their feathers and splashing through all the puddles whilst loudly proclaiming their delight. In the distance, Mel could just make out activity at the canal site. Evidently, the navvies didn't intend to lose another day's pay.

Josh cantered up on his big black gelding. John emerged from the sheds to greet him.

'Morning Mel, morning, John. I just called to see how you fared after the storm,' he called, hitching his horse to the gatepost.

'Not too bad, apart from mud everywhere. It's good of you to look in,' John told him.

Mel frowned at Josh. She found him difficult to understand. One minute he was all consideration, the next he was lashing out without a thought. Which was the real Josh – the perfect gentleman or the hard-hearted peer? Although her heart told her to trust him, her past experience of the upper classes told her to be wary, especially as she'd already discovered that, similar to many of his contemporaries, he sneered at anyone in trade. She knew she'd be wise to keep her heart intact, but . . . She sighed.

Suddenly they noticed someone hurrying across the field.

'Isn't that one of the navvies coming this way?' Josh queried. 'He seems to be in a hurry. There could be trouble at the canal site.'

The man reached the gate, gasping for breath.

'Is Mr. Johnson here? There's been a landslide. A large part of the canal wall has collapsed, trapping several of the men. We need help getting them out,' he wheezed.

'Mel, you run and see if the engineer is indoors. John and I will go on over and see if we can help,' Josh said, naturally taking command. As Mel raced upstairs to find Rupert, her thoughts were with Connor. Was he alright? Was he one of the ones trapped in the mud? Mel feared that might well be the case, as it was usually Connor who was the one to contact the engineer. Bursting into the engineer's bedroom which he also used as an office, Mel quickly reported the bad news. With a harassed look, he ran his fingers through his hair and groaned.

'This is all I need,' he sighed. 'I just hope there are no fatalities. It makes so much paperwork.'

As he hurried off downstairs, Mel stared after him, speechless. How could he? People could be dying and all he could think about was the extra paperwork he'd have to do. Then she too went back downstairs, wondering if it would be possible for her to go to the site. She wanted to know if Connor was alright. She just couldn't bear to think of those mischievous black eyes being closed forever. Her aunt told her she must stay here, ready to receive the injured if necessary. But it was torture not knowing. How long would she have to wait?

CHAPTER 6

As the two men galloped off across the fields, Ben came round the corner of the barn.

'What's up?' he asked. 'Where are Dad and Josh off to in such a hurry?'

There's been a landslide at the canal site. All this rain has brought part of the canal wall down, trapping several navvies. Your dad's gone to help.'

'If they are bringing the injured back here, I'd best take the wagon over.' He hurried off to harness up Captain.

'Why bring them back here and not take them straight to their camp?' Mel asked her aunt.

'It only consists of basic huts and as most of the men are single, it's better that they are brought here first to be cleaned up. Also, I can treat a lot of minor injuries as I have a wide knowledge of herbal remedies. But first, hot water. Run and put the kettle and a pan of water on the range, there's a good girl. Then we'll get the copper going. After that, I must check my store of herbal tinctures and salves.'

As Mel bustled about filling kettles and pans, she couldn't help being intrigued about the herbal remedies that her aunt used. She followed her into a small room off the dairy that she hadn't been in before. Shelves reached up to the ceiling, and were filled with bottles and jars of all colours.

'Don't stand there gawping, lass.' Hannah handed her a basket. 'I need to prepare some fresh herb poultices for their wounds and bruises. Come out to the herb garden and I'll show you what to pick.' Then, having identified the plants that she required—comfrey, potentilla, calendula, yarrow, rosemary and lavender—she left Mel to it whilst she prepared other tinctures in her still room. Relishing in the aromas of the various herbs, Mel quickly filled her basket. Back indoors, her aunt handed her a mortar and pestle with instructions to pound the leaves she'd picked into a pulp, adding a little water and honey to bind them together to use as poultices.

'Does this really work?' Mel didn't stop mixing but she was intrigued to know more about its benefits.

'Oh, yes, country folk have used herbs for medicinal purposes for years,' Hannah told her. 'Certain herbs are good for healing open wounds and others for bruising and sprains. I was lucky. Lady Benchard senior gave me an old book on herbal recipes. She told me that, as the present Lady Benchard wasn't interested, she thought I'd make better use of it. I must admit I find it fascinating and very helpful. It's surprising what small injuries and ailments occur on a farm. I keep a wide variety of dried herbs as well as using fresh ones.'

'What's in those coloured bottles?'

'I make up a range of tinctures to keep for things like coughs, headaches and such, as well as salves for bruises and insect bites.'

Mel flicked through the book. The list of herbs and the amounts to use reminded her of the business books she used to help her father with. She felt a frisson of excitement. Maybe this was something she could really get involved in.

'Will you teach me what's what and how to mix them?' Mel asked.

'I'd love to, but I can hear the men coming back. It's time to put it into practice.'

Mel rushed outside, eager for news of Connor. She paled at the sight of those poor men, covered in mud and blood. Anxiously she searched their faces, but she couldn't see any sign of Connor. Where was he? Was he alright? She must ask Josh. But Josh and her uncle were already carrying buckets of water from the pump to swill the worst of the mud away. Her aunt called to her.

'Quickly girl, don't just stand there. Fetch me those poultices we've prepared. Can't you see these men are in pain?'

After watching how it was done, she helped Hannah cover the cleaned wounds with the herbal mixture. For those that only had bad bruises, Hannah smoothed some of her arnica ointment onto the darkening patches. Another wagonload of men was brought in.

Hannah turned to her niece. 'At this rate, we shall need more poultices. Mel, go quickly and pick some more comfrey leaves, yarrow and lavender. It will help stop the swelling.'

As Mel grabbed up a basket from the kitchen, Josh came in for a kettle of water.

'Josh, have you seen Connor yet?' she asked. 'Is he alright?'

'I don't know who this Connor is?' Josh paused. 'Or do I? Perhaps he's the navvy you were cuddling on the ground the day I rode by.'

'No, we . . .'

'You didn't need to sink that low. If you're so desperate, I'm always willing to oblige.' He pulled her hard into his arms.

Mel gasped in shock, her heart beating a rapid tattoo against his chest. Then his mouth descended on hers. But this was no lover's kiss. It was a brutal, punishing kiss. Then, as he abruptly released her, she staggered back.

'You're despicable, Josh Benchard,' she spat out, her eyes blazing.

When he laughed, Mel raised her hand to slap his face. But he had already turned away, walking out of the door. Trembling with fury, she headed for the herb garden. But this time, even picking the comfrey and thyme leaves didn't have their usual calming effect. Back in the still room, as Mel pounded the herbs, she imagined it was Josh she was pounding.

'My, who are you trying to kill?' her aunt asked, coming into the room. 'From the expression on your face, I think it's just as well that person isn't here.'

Mel blushed. 'It's not like that, it's just seeing all those poor men injured.'

But Hannah just shook her head. 'Yes, well, mix in some honey and water into those herbs and let's get some more poultices on them.'

Pulling herself together, Mel quickly completed her job and helped her aunt attend to the final group of men.

Finally, all the men had been attended to and settled as comfortably as possible on the hay in the barn, where they were to stay the night. John and Ben went off to tend to the animals. Hannah and Mel retired to the kitchen to prepare the evening meal, including a large pan of broth for the injured men. Mel had been hoping to ask Rupert Johnson about Connor, but he didn't turn up for the meal, and Josh had ridden off some time ago. So she had to go to bed not knowing anything new.

The following morning, Mel was prepared to help her aunt renew the poultices on the most seriously injured men. Ben took the others back to their camp so that those who were able could get back to work. The canal must still be dug and no work meant no wages.

'I think you know enough to be able to continue here without me,' her aunt said. 'And the men prefer you to tend them. They say you've softer hands. But don't allow any liberties, mind.'

'But what if I do it wrong?' Mel was nervous.

'You can do it. Just replace the poultice with the same as those you take off. It would be a great help to me, dear, as I didn't get much other work done yesterday.'

Soon, with the grateful encouragement from her patients, Mel's confidence grew, and she found herself enjoying it. For the first time since she'd left her home in Birmingham, she felt as though life had a purpose again. She was determined to learn more about this craft. The only thing marring her horizon was the fact that she couldn't discover the whereabouts of Connor. What could have happened to him? No one that she asked had seen him, but one of the navvies that she questioned just said, "Tell him to watch his back". When she'd asked what he meant, he refused to elaborate. Did this mean he was in danger? Why and from whom, she couldn't even begin to guess.

For the next few days, Mel looked after her patients while her aunt got on with the general work of running a farm. She felt that she'd found her niche at last and every spare minute she studied Hannah's old book of herbs and their properties. She was amazed at how many things they were used for. After the rest of the men had left for the canal site, life at the farm returned to normal. But Hannah still managed to find time to teach Mel how to make the various tinctures and salves needed to replenish her reserve ready for any other crisis. She also showed her how to mix rosemary and lavender essential oils to add to the water when bathing or washing hair. Mel was kept busy and the days flew by. She still worried about the absence of any news of Connor. Also, she was surprised that Fleur hadn't been to see her. She really thought she'd intended to be a friend, but obviously she too was busy doing other things.

Two days later, her uncle announced he was taking two calves to Gloucester market and asked if anyone would like to come along. Both Hannah and Mel jumped at the chance of a day out, and hurried to find their bonnets and shawls.

'It will give us chance to buy some material to make a couple more dresses for you, my dear,' Hannah said.

Mel chewed at her lip. 'Oh, but I have only a few coppers left. I don't think that will stretch to clothes.'

'Don't worry about that. You deserve something for all the work you've done since you arrived. Come on, we mustn't keep John waiting.'

Soon the three of them were wedged together on the front seat of the wagon, pulled by Captain, with the calves bawling for their mothers behind them. The weather was pleasantly warm and Mel lifted her face to the sun with delight. After the trauma of the last week, it felt wonderful to be out, especially with the anticipation of buying cloth for new clothes ahead. As they neared the town, the roads became busier. Hannah waved to two neighbouring farmers' wives carrying heavy baskets filled with home-made cheeses and decorated butter pats. There were carts piled high with fruit and vegetables. Even a man and two young boys driving a gaggle of waddling geese. As they neared the town and the streets lined with houses, Mel felt a stab of homesickness for her old life. Suddenly she felt the familiar bubbling up of anger towards her father for leaving her like he did. She gave a sob, but quickly stifled it as her aunt turned to her with a worried look.

They had reached Westgate Street, which was already lined with rows of merchants' stalls. John let them off, promising to meet up with them again at the Golden Fleece Inn for lunch, before continuing on to Eastgate Street. Here, pens had been set up, and farmers and drovers were milling around them, prodding pigs and cattle, examining horses' teeth and hooves, and haggling over the prices. The volume of noise from the animals and the men's shouts increasing throughout the day. Hannah and Mel enjoyed browsing through the various stalls. They both purchased some bolts of sturdy cotton in blue and green to make into summer dresses, also buttons and thread to match.

'Now, Mel, you must buy some material for your riding outfit for when Josh teaches you to ride.' Mel shook her head.

'No, I'm sure he's too busy to bother with me. Anyway, I'm not sure that I want to learn to ride,' Mel added. 'I'm happy just using the dog cart if I need to go further than I can walk.'

'Rubbish,' Hannah said 'You're a country girl now, Mel. Riding a horse is expected of you.'

'I really think it would be a waste of money, Aunt Hannah. If necessary I can always alter one of my black town dresses. I doubt I shall wear them again as they are. Oh, look over there.' She grabbed her aunt's arm. 'Isn't that Fleur talking to someone? I haven't seen her lately. I must go and have a word with her.' But before she could cross the road, Fleur's companion turned round. It was Rupert Johnson. As the engineer caught sight of them, he said something to Fleur and they both hurried off in the opposite direction. Mel felt the delight of the day slip away.

'Oh, aunt, why did she cut me? Do you think I've offended her?'

'No, dear, I'm sure it was just because she was with Rupert. In fact, thinking about it, I don't think Fleur even noticed you.

I think the engineer purposely hurried her off in the opposite direction because he didn't want us to see them together. You must admit, it looks a bit suspicious. I wonder if Josh knows of this. But then again, we might be reading too much into what could well be an accidental meeting.'

Mel frowned. 'I don't know. I've seen them together a couple of times now. But I wouldn't want to make trouble by telling Josh. I'm sure Fleur wouldn't do anything too stupid, would she?'

'Let's hope not. Now come along, it's time to make our way to the Golden Fleece or John will be wondering where we are.'

'What's that tower over there?' Mel asked. Her aunt looked across and smiled.

'That's Gloucester cathedral. We haven't got time today, but one day I'll show you around. It's well worth a visit.'

Suddenly there was a commotion behind them – people screaming and shouting.

'Look out!' someone yelled. 'A bullock's got loose from the market pens.'

The scene down the street was one of chaos. People falling into stalls in their panic, spilling their contents across the street. Women snatching up children, while men, with shouts and sticks, tried unsuccessfully to get the crazed animal back under control. The crowd was surging down the street towards Mel and her aunt.

'Quick, grab my hand and let's try and make it into the Golden Fleece,' Hannah said. But even as she reached out, a fat man with his wig askew, who was looking back at the pandemonium instead of where he was going, tripped and, arms rotating frantically, cannoned into Hannah, bringing them both crashing to the ground, his waistcoat buttons bursting free like pebbles from a slingshot. One of the buttons hit

Mel on the side of her neck just as she was bending down to help her aunt. She stumbled back in shock and slipped on the cobbles, falling on top of the fat man. As they all struggled to free themselves, the lethal clatter of the beast's hooves was getting even nearer.

Suddenly a man in ragged clothes limped forward from the crowd and lifted Mel to her feet, and then proceeded to help Hannah up. A second, similarly dressed man joined them and they ushered the stunned ladies to the safety of the pub's doorway. The fat man just managed to roll aside as the escaped animal thundered past. It had been a close shave.

'Are you OK, Mrs. P? Miss Mel?' The limping man asked.

'Yes, thanks to you both. It was very brave. You might have been killed yourselves, especially with a bad leg,' Hannah said.

Mel looked closely at her rescuers. 'Why, you were among the navvies injured in that canal accident?' she exclaimed.

They nodded.

'That's right. Reckon you saved our lives then, so we couldn't leave you in the path of that crazed animal, could we?' He grinned.

John came puffing up to them.

'Are you both alright? I was so worried. When that bullock got out I didn't know where you were.'

'We're both fine,' Hannah assured him 'Thanks to these two young men.' Her husband looked at the two navvies in surprise. 'They came forward and pulled us out of the way despite their injuries, which is more than could be said for other folk. Even those that consider themselves superior to these lads.'

John shook their hands. 'You have my eternal thanks. Come in and let me buy you a meal.'

They shook their heads.

'Thanks but no, it wouldn't look right—us sitting down to eat with you. But a pint of ale wouldn't go down badly, out here on this bench.'

While John went in to buy the lads their ale, Hannah and Mel sank gratefully onto the adjoining bench, still very shaken from their experience. When her uncle came back with the drinks, he asked the navvies how come they were in town. The men told them that as they hadn't recovered enough from their injuries yet to work, they'd come here hoping to find out more news about their mate, Connor O'Flynn.

Mel looked up with interest. 'Do you know where he is,' she asked. 'Is he alright?'

'We know where he is, but that's all. You see, he's in prison. He was arrested on the day of the accident.'

Mel gasped. 'I can't believe it. I took him to be an honest man.'

'Connor hasn't a dishonest bone in his body.'

'Then why was he arrested?'

'Those in charge accused him of sabotaging the works and causing the landslide.'

'But I understood it was caused by the amount of rain we've had,' John said.

'It was, and also because the engineers had misjudged the lay of the land. But rather than admit to their mistake, they blamed Connor. Especially as he was our spokesman and stood up for our rights. The bosses saw their chance to rid themselves of a thorn in their sides as well as the opportunity to shift the blame of the accident.'

Mel bristled with anger. 'But that's unfair. We must do something.'

Sadly, the navvies shook their heads.

'There's not much we can do. It's our word against them, and they won't listen to the likes of us.'

'Then we must find someone to speak for you. Perhaps Josh would?' Hannah suggested.

Mel doubted it. She remembered how he had once referred to Connor as 'scum'. But who else was there? She would have to persuade him. It was unthinkable that an innocent man should be locked up merely for trying to help his fellow workers.

'We'll look into it and see if there's anything we can do,' John promised them. 'But now I must get these ladies to their dinner before they faint away with hunger.'

CHAPTER 7

That night, Mel couldn't sleep. She kept thinking of Connor, shut up in a dank, smelly prison cell, for something that wasn't his fault. She'd only met him briefly, but his cheeky grin and mischievous twinkling eyes had left a lasting impression on her. As had his kindness to her when she had been feeling so low. All her instincts told her that he was a good person. Previously, he had mentioned he'd voluntarily taken on the job of spokesman for the navvies, acting as a go-between for them with the bosses. Also, he was always chasing Rupert up to keep abreast of his duties, which upset the engineer. Was he the person who had brought the false charges against Connor? Maybe she would try and talk to Rupert Johnson.

Being too restless to lie in bed, she got up, wrapped a shawl around her shoulders, and leaned out of the window. The light was fading from the evening sky, darkening it from rosy lavender in the west through hues of purple and blue to velvet black off in the east. Not a single cloud obscured the view. When she had first arrived, she had been afraid of the night sky. It had seemed so immense, limitless without any buildings to break it up. Like some great ocean ready to swallow her up. It had made her feel tiny, insignificant, of no consequence whatsoever. But during her time here, she'd become used to all these vast empty spaces. Now its peaceful beauty seemed to welcome her, soothing her like some unexpected friend. She suddenly realized that she was changing. This place was beginning to feel like home, and the people were now like old friends. She was determined to help them however she could. As the black velvet finally swallowed up the sky's remaining colour, Mel returned to her bed and was soon fast asleep.

The following day Mel sought out Rupert, but the engineer was proving very difficult to pin down. It was almost as though he was anticipating Mel's questions. Questions that he was not prepared to answer. She realized that her only option now was to persuade Josh to help Connor. But would he consider it beneath him to help the 'scum'?

Two days later, Mel decided that if she was going to get help for Connor, she was going to have to pluck up the courage to pay a visit to the manor and ask to speak to Josh. Having begged a couple of hours free from her aunt, she donned her shawl and sturdy boots for the walk across the fields. It was such a lovely day that it was good to be outdoors. The sky was a periwinkle blue with small, fluffy clouds along the horizon. It put Mel in the mind of a child having spilt a box of cotton wool balls during its walk. But the only cloud on Mel's horizon was the thought of Connor's cheerful face shut up in that awful prison. She was sure it was for something he didn't do. Connor only tried to help people. She just had to persuade Josh to use his influence.

She was just leaving the farmyard when the geese started up their usual noisy warning with which they always greeted visitors. Pausing, she looked up to see two horsemen coming her way, soon recognising the riders as Josh and Fleur. Fleur reminded Mel of a princess in her royal blue riding costume and her fair hair. In contrast, Josh was more like the devil himself on his big black stallion and dressed all in black. At the sight of him, Mel's heart did a rapid stutter and then gathered speed. Though why the sight of his stern, angular face and ice-blue eyes should have this effect on her she just couldn't understand.

'Hello Josh, I was coming to see you. Fleur, how are you? I was beginning to think . . .' But before Mel could say anything more, Fleur interrupted.

'Hello Mel, Josh is going to teach you to ride. Now, you must excuse me. I have to see Hannah.' Then she was off her pony and disappearing into the farmhouse. Mel stared at her in surprise. Josh dismounted and tied both animals to the gatepost.

'I rather think that's Fleur's way of getting out of some awkward explaining,' he said, patting his horse. 'She's been disappearing rather a lot lately. She says she's been visiting you. But judging from this meeting, I'm not entirely convinced.'

Mel frowned. She hadn't seen her friend for some time. In fact, the last time was at the market when she'd been with Rupert Johnson. But she was not about to tell tales.

'It's kind of you to offer to teach me to ride, Josh,' she said, changing the subject. 'But I wouldn't want to take up your time. I'm sure you've more important things to do.' *Like getting Connor out of jail*, she thought.

'I wouldn't have offered if I didn't have time.'

'But I don't really want to learn,' she told him, eyeing the horses with trepidation.

'Of course you do. Everyone rides in the country. I have a nice quiet mare in the stables that would suit you admirably. I'll bring her round in the morning.'

'No, please, I've nothing suitable to wear. I was going to alter one of my old town dresses but haven't had time. Maybe when I've finished it,' she added, hoping to delay the ordeal.

'No problem. You can borrow one of my mother's old riding dresses. She's about your size.' As Mel shook her head, he continued, 'Mother doesn't ride anymore due to health problems, so she won't mind you borrowing one. I'll be here tomorrow morning, complete with horse, side-saddle and outfit. Everything you'll need.'

Mel gasped. 'You mean I'll have to sit on one of those things,' she said, pointing to Fleur's side-saddle. 'Oh no, there's no way you'll ever get me up onto that. It doesn't look at all safe.'

'Don't be silly. They are perfectly safe. All ladies use them.'

'Not me. Anyway, I'm not a lady. As you have pointed out, our family was 'trade'. So that rules me out.'

'Now you're being childish. Your father was once wealthy, albeit a merchant. So you must have been brought up as a lady.'

'If you mean did I spend all my time drinking tea and going to balls, then you're wrong. After my mother died, I spent all my time with Papa at his works. I even kept his books for him until his. . . .' Tears clogged her throat as she remembered those last days.

'A very unconventional upbringing for a girl. But that doesn't mean it's right for you to career around the countryside astride like some urchin. The side-saddle isn't that hard to manage.'

'Have you ever ridden side-saddle?' she asked him.

'Actually, no, but if it was difficult ladies wouldn't use them, would they.'

Even though she wanted him to think well of her, she just couldn't bring herself to attempt it. She was still scared of horses, but she wasn't going to admit that to Josh. It was one thing to help groom one of the farm horses that Ben called 'gentle giants'. It was quite another to sit up on one of these spirited creatures, especially on the contraption they called a side-saddle.

'Well, here's one 'lady' who won't be even trying, thank you very much. I'll stick to walking.'

'It's not like you to give up on anything. Look how well you coped helping out with the canal accident.'

'That was different. That time I had both my feet on firm ground.'

'I rather hoped you'd learn to ride so that you could accompany Fleur to wherever she goes. Make sure she doesn't meet the wrong people.'

Mel felt a pang of disappointment. Josh hadn't been thinking of her at all, but was trying to use her. That's why he wanted her to ride side-saddle. Not because he thought she was a lady, but because he wanted her to look like a suitable companion to ride beside his sister.

'I'm sorry, but I am not a babysitter,' she told him bitterly.

'I didn't mean . . .' But whatever he was going to say was lost as Fleur bounced back, injecting her usual fluffy nonsense into the conversation.

'Morning Mr Benchard, Ladies.' The Blacksmith had stopped beside them.

'You look worried, Mr Strong, Is everything alright?' Josh asked. The blacksmith shook his head and sighed.

'It's my daughter, Sarah. I don't suppose you've seen her on your travels?'

There was a general shaking of heads.

'I'm worried,' he continued. 'You see, yesterday morning we had a bit of a row. She flounced out in anger and hasn't been home since. I was certain she'd come back that night and we could talk things over calmly, but there's been no sign of her.'

'I'm sure she's alright, Mr Strong. She's probably stayed with friends overnight,' Josh reassured him.

'She hasn't got many friends. She's a bit of a loner. That's the trouble. She's been spending a lot of her time with those canal navvies. And now she's in the family way. That's what the row was about. I was just going over to the canal site now to see if anyone's seen her.' He sighed. 'Oh, I wish the wretched canal hadn't been built near our village. Life will never be the same again.'

'Don't worry, we'll scout around the area and see if we can find out anything. Come along, Fleur.' As Josh turned his horse around, Fleur looked from Josh to Mel.

'But I thought you were going to arrange for Mel to learn to ride?' she said.

'The lady has declined the offer. Now come on,' he called over his shoulder as he cantered away.

Fleur gave Mel a puzzled look. Then, with a wave, she was off after her brother. The blacksmith was already striding purposely off in the direction of the canal. Mel was furious. Josh hadn't even said goodbye. Then she realised that Josh had spent so much time trying to browbeat her into those riding lessons that he hadn't given her any opportunity to bring up the subject of freeing Connor. Now she was back to square one. Furious, she headed back to the farmhouse to look for her aunt. She found her in the dairy, churning the butter.

'Hello, Mel.' Hannah let go of the handle and straightened her back. 'This butter is taking a long time to turn today. At this rate, I shall have to find a silver crown to put in it. That usually does the trick.'

'Let me have a go. Aunt Hannah, I need some way of working off my frustration.'

As she relinquished her place at the butter churn, Hannah asked her niece, 'You been arguing with Josh again?'

'Oh, Aunt Hannah, why does every conversation we have end like this?'

'You must remember, you had a very unusual upbringing. The ladies in Josh's world are taught to be meek and polite and never argue with a gentleman. He's just not used to someone like you.'

'Never! But surely ladies must sometimes disagree with the gentleman!'

'Yes, they probably do, but they would never tell him so. It's considered bad etiquette.'

'How ridiculous. But you often disagree with Uncle John. I've heard you.'

'Ah, but it's different for us lesser mortals. Though even then, it's the men who always make the final decisions. At least they think they do! There are times when us women have to use a bit of guile. You'd do well to remember that.'

'Josh wanted me to ride side-saddle and I was too scared.' She finally admitted.

'Ah!'

'Do you ride, Aunt Hannah?' Mel asked.

Her aunt shook her head. 'Not now. I did as a child but that was astride. I'm afraid I never did master the side-saddle.'

'Josh said everyone has to ride in the country. How do you manage?'

'That's easy, my dear. I drive myself in the pony and trap.'

'Oh, Aunt, you're a genius.' She gave her aunt a mischievous smile. 'I'll just ask Josh to teach me to drive a pony and trap. Oh, by the way, the Blacksmith stopped by when we were talking, asking if we'd seen his daughter.' Mel said, changing the subject. 'Evidently, she ran off after a row with her dad and hasn't been home since.'

'That Sarah always was a bit flighty. Takes after her mother, I reckon.'

'I don't think I've met Mrs. Strong.'

'No, and you won't. She up and left when Sarah was just a scrap of a babe. Ran off with a travelling pedlar. It wasn't easy for Eli Strong – bringing up a young girl on his own. I hope the silly girl hasn't gone and done something stupid.'

Mel fell silent, trying to think what she would do if she was in Sarah's shoes. She must feel desperate with no one to turn to for help. The sloshing of the butter-milk had turned to a heavier bumping.

'Ah good, by the sound of it, that butter is ready,' said her aunt. 'Bring the wooden pats over and we'll just shape it into smaller blocks.'

They finished the job in companionable silence.

In the afternoon, Hannah persuaded her niece to go out for a walk while the fine weather lasted. Mel decided to walk down towards the canal site to see if there had been any sightings of the Blacksmith's daughter. On the other side of the orchard, she came across Ruth at her easel, painting the scene with the canal workings in the background. Having greeted each other warmly, Mel admired the painting.

'I felt I had to capture the scene because it will soon be gone completely. A fleeting incident in life,' Ruth explained.

'Not fleeting enough for many who live around here,' Mel laughed. She studied the painting. 'That's very good. You really make it come alive. I wish I could do that.'

'Give it a try. I have some spare paper here.' Ruth carefully removed her own painting from the easel, replacing it with a clean sheet. But Mel's efforts were very shaky in places and stick-like in others. She grimaced.

'A three-year-old could do better. I could never master it.'

'Didn't you have watercolour lessons when you lived in Birmingham?' Ruth asked. 'I thought all well-to-do ladies were taught drawing and painting, along with embroidery and dancing classes.'

'I didn't have any of that. Anyway, I found I had a natural aptitude for figures, so I persuaded Papa to let me help him with the accounts. Not very useful training for a gentleman's wife,' she said, thinking fleetingly of Josh, before pushing the notion firmly from her mind. 'No, I'll leave the painting to you. But don't you feel nervous, being out here on your own?'

Ruth shook her head. 'No, I like being on my own so that I can concentrate on my art. The men never bother me. I need to do something with my life. It will be different when Ben and I are married. I shall be busy helping him then.'

'Have you set a date yet?'

'Ben's not in any hurry. I think it's the problem of us having to live with his parents when we're married. It wouldn't be ideal but then again, I don't want us to have to wait for them to retire or something. That could be years away. Oh Mel, sometimes I wonder if Ben really wants to get married. Does he love me enough?'

'Of course he does. Don't worry, something will turn up, you'll see. I'm going to walk down towards the workings. See you later.'

As Mel made her way across the fields her mind was on Sarah, wondering where the blacksmith's daughter could have gone. Her father said he'd tried all the people she may have stayed with but had no luck. Could she really have spent the night with one of the navvies? As she got nearer to the site she gasped in amazement. It was huge, much larger than it had seemed from a distance. Also, far wider than the canals she remembered in her home town of Birmingham. She was sure it must be deeper too. Hundreds of men were swarming over it. Some with pick-axes breaking up the bed of the canal site, others shovelling the broken soil into wooden wheelbarrows. More men wheeled the barrows along narrow wooden planks before attaching them to pulleys, operated by men and horses up on the banks to lift the unwanted soil out of the way. And so the circle continued. It was a scene of non-stop activity. There was a constant buzz of noise; a mixture of men's shouts, and the thuds, scrapes and squeaks of their tools. Mel had planned to talk to some of the navvies to discover when Sarah had last been seen. Also, to see if they could shed any light on why Connor had been arrested. But she could see it would be impossible to attract their attention, much less talk to them. She was just turning away when Rupert Johnson approached her.

'What are you doing here? Still poking your nose in other people's business?' he sneered.

'I was just going for a walk. There's no law against that, is there? I was wondering if there had been any sightings of Sarah.'

'Not round here, there hasn't. And don't you go wasting the men's time with your pointless questioning. Time's money in this job, I'll have you know.'

'I am aware of that. I'm not the feather-brain you think I am.'

'Well, you want to watch your step, Miss Know-it-all, or you could find yourself regretting it.' He waved his finger in her face.

'Are you threatening me, Mr Johnson?'

'Me – threatening you? Whatever gives you that idea? I'm merely offering you some friendly advice.' He smirked, before turning his back on her and walking off.

Mel shivered. Had it been intended as a threat or was it really just friendly advice? She wasn't sure. The man always managed to make her feel uncomfortable. There was just something about him she didn't trust. A cloud covered the sun, and looking up, she realised there was a bank of black clouds gathering on the horizon. There seemed to be a storm gathering. She hoped it wasn't an omen.

CHAPTER 8

The following day saw Mel happily helping her aunt in the still room. While Hannah replenished her stock of hand cream and healing salves, Mel prepared both lavender and rosemary waters used for washing hair. They were both startled when Ben burst into the room.

'The blacksmith and Josh are getting up a search party to look for his daughter, and Dad and I are joining them. So we may be late in for meals,' he explained.

Hannah sighed. 'Oh dear, I hope they find her,' she said.

Ben shook his head. 'It's my belief that she's run off with her boyfriend and they're probably miles away by now.'

'Well, either way, it will probably help to put Mr Strong's mind at rest. I'll keep something cold for you when you need it.'

Then Ben was gone, slamming the door behind him.

Hannah and Mel were on tenterhooks all day, waiting for news of the search. At last, just as it was getting dusk, Ben came back.

'They've found her,' he told them.

'Where?' the girls asked.

'Face down in the little pond behind that old derelict bothy in the corner of the manor gardens.'

'Was she murdered?' Hannah asked.

'Who knows? There were no marks to show that any violence had been used. So we don't know if she was pushed or chose to drown herself, or even if she fell in accidentally. Maybe we will never know. Anyway, the men came back to fetch a door and will then carry her to Mr Strong's cottage.'

'Oh, the poor girl, and poor Mr Strong. He's got no one now. Well, I'd best be gathering up my bits and pieces and then I'll be getting over there,' Hannah said. 'I do all the laying out for the village,' she explained for Mel's benefit.

* * *

The next day was Sunday and the church was full. Everyone had turned up in deference to poor Sarah. Her father was there, but he was a shadow of his former self, as though he hadn't slept for a week. During the service, the vicar announced that Sarah's funeral would be on Tuesday.

'Where's she being buried?' someone asked.

'Right here in the churchyard, next to the rest of her family,' the blacksmith stated firmly.

'But suicides aren't allowed to be buried in holy ground,' came back the reply.

'As we have no proof that it was suicide, we are giving her the benefit of the doubt and treating it as an accident,' the vicar explained.

'T'was murder,' the blacksmith burst out. 'T'was one of those filthy canal navvies, mark my word. If I ever find out which one, I'll beat the living daylights out of him.'

Rupert Johnson leapt to his feet. 'You can't go flinging accusations about like that. It could have been anyone.'

'Oh yes, and who else is it likely to be?' Strong also stood up, pointing his finger at the engineer. 'Maybe it was you. You're not as green as you look. I've seen you sniffing round ladies' skirts.'

'Don't be ridiculous. You'll be accusing Josh Benchard next. After all, the bothy where she was found was in his family's garden,' Rupert shouted back.

'Gentlemen, gentlemen, please remember you're in the house of our Lord.' Rev. Crosley flapped his hands franticly, before mopping the sweat off his podgy red face. 'I've never known such conduct. At least keep your disagreements until you are outside. Thank you,' he added, as both men sank sheepishly back into their seats. In the ensuing silence, he continued, 'Now, let us pray.'

After the service, as the people filed out into the churchyard, it was soon obvious that not only had the argument continued, but several other local farmers had joined in. Words like missing sheep and broken fences were banded around. The engineer, looking very harassed, seemed to be looking for an escape route. Josh was also determined not to be drawn into the discussion and headed for his carriage. But before he could alight, someone grabbed his arm. Shocked, he looked down his nose at the offending appendage, only to discover it was Mel's small but determined hand that clutched at him. He could feel the urgency in it, and looked into those pleading chocolate eyes in surprise. Their disagreement over the riding lessons was forgotten in the need to learn what was troubling her.

'Miss Meredith – Mel – what's wrong?'

'Please help. You're the only one I know to ask. Can you

get Connor O'Flynn released from prison? I'm sure he's not done anything to warrant his arrest.'

Josh's expression turned to disgust. 'You want my help to free your Irish lover-boy? You've got a nerve!'

'No, you've got it wrong. He's not my lover-boy, and I'm not asking this because it benefits me.'

'Explain,' he demanded curtly.

'Connor is the unofficial spokesman for the canal navvies. They respect him as they know he will do his best to get their needs met. For one thing, I know he always used to chase the engineer to make sure they always got their wages on time. But since he's been in prison, the men have got restless. I've heard the local farmers complaining of things going missing and now these suspicions of murder. Well, I'm worried about what will happen next,' she finished, slightly out of breath in her haste to make Josh understand.

He frowned. 'I see your point. Well, I will look into it, but I can't promise anything. My father is the local magistrate so he may be able to throw some light on the situation. Until we know why he was thrown into prison, we can't do anything. But leave it in my hands and stop worrying.' With a pat on her hand, he turned and disappeared into his carriage.

Mel sighed. There was nothing more she could do but wait and hope that Josh kept his word.

'Are you coming, Mel?' her uncle called. We must be getting back. There's work waiting to do.' Mel tried to put the worry of Connor out of her mind as she joined the others for the walk back to the farm.

It rained on the day of Sarah's funeral. Only a small, sodden group of people were there to see her being lowered into her grave. Many parishioners were still not happy that she had been allowed to be buried in hallowed ground. Mel noticed that several navvies stood beneath the dripping trees on the perimeter of the churchyard, caps in hand and heads bowed. Surely, Mel thought, if they had been involved with her death—accidental or otherwise—they wouldn't be there! Would anyone ever know the truth?

At the farm, things slipped back into the usual routine. Days went by and Mel didn't hear anything from Josh. Had he made any progress? Or had he just forgotten about it? She wished she had some way of finding out. But she hadn't set eyes on him since the church service. She hadn't had a chance to speak to Fleur either, though she thought she'd caught a glimpse of her with Rupert Johnson the other evening. Mel worried about her friend. She seemed to be getting far too friendly with the engineer, and she could see nothing good coming from it.

At the weekend, Ben asked his mother if she would bake one of her special plum cakes as he'd invited Ruth to tea. His mother was delighted to do so, and no one was really surprised when they announced their engagement.

'About time too,' his father told them. 'I reckon this calls for the opening of one of your Mother's bottles of elderberry wine.' So, with many congratulations and much backslapping, everyone toasted the happy couple.

'It's good to have something cheerful to celebrate for a change,' Hannah said.

'I'm so pleased for you, Ruth, but what changed your mind?' Mel asked. 'The last time we spoke, you seemed to think it would be some time before you both tied the knot.'

'Lord Benchard.' At the surprised looks, she explained. 'He has offered to rent us Hollowtree Cottage.'

'Isn't that where the Simmons live?' John asked.

'Lived,' Ben corrected. 'Old Simmons can't get around as well as he used to so they have decided to go and live with their daughter and her husband in Gloucester. Lord Benchard retired him a long time ago but allowed him to stay on in the cottage, and as it hadn't been used by a worker for some time, it was surplus to the estate's needs. He said it would be better rented out than left empty. Evidently, houses soon deteriorate if left empty for long periods.'

'It's ideal. Still close enough for you to help your father on the farm,' Hannah pointed out.

'Yes and if I remember rightly, it's got a decent-sized garden and a pigsty attached, so you'll be able to be at least partly self-sufficient,' John told the couple.

'Have you set a date for the wedding?' Mel asked. She was surprised at the change she saw in Ruth. It was as though a light had been switched on inside her as she caught Ben's adoring gaze focused on her. Her blue eyes were sparkling with excitement and her usually pale face was enhanced with a becoming blush. Even her hair seemed to reflect that golden glow. Ben looked at his father.

'We thought about six weeks' time, just before we have to start haymaking, if that's alright with you. That will give the Simmons's plenty of time to move their things out, and for us to get it spruced up a bit. We wondered if we could use the barn for the party afterwards, Dad?' Ben asked. , 'Before it gets filled with hay, of course.'

Everyone laughed and John readily gave his permission. Mel congratulated her friend.

'This must have been a surprise. The last time we spoke of it, you seemed resigned to a long wait,' she added quietly.

'It's a wonderful surprise.' Ruth admitted. ''I'd quite resigned myself to several more years of waiting. The offer of this cottage is like a dream come true. I never imagined the old lord would even consider letting the cottage to us.' She suddenly gripped Mel's arm. 'I'm scared it's too good to be true. That I will wake up and find it's all a dream.'

'I'm sure you've nothing to worry about. After all, what could possibly go wrong?' Mel reassured her friend. She thought that the offer of the cottage was probably Josh's idea, and she felt her heart warm with thanks. He may act cold and haughty at times but she was sure that underneath he was kind and considerate.

Ruth took Mel's hand. 'Will you be my bridesmaid, Mel?'

'Are you sure?' Mel asked. 'I've only been here a few months.'

'I know, but I've always felt you understood me. It would mean a lot to me if you would.'

Mel was touched. 'In that case, I'd be honoured,' she said, hugging her friend. Then Hannah and the two girls went into a huddle, discussing dresses, colours, and other wedding details. As Ruth hadn't a mother to help her, Hannah had offered to do what she could, which surprised Mel as she always thought she had reservations about Ruth. But it seemed that now things had been finalised, she'd decided to accept her. When the chatter about wedding dresses and such had died down, Ben stood up.

'Come on, Ruth,' he said. 'It's time I took you home. It looks like it's going to rain soon.'

Ruth slipped her shawl around her shoulders and took Ben's arm. 'Thank you all for a lovely meal. I'm so pleased you're happy for us,' she told them as they left, her cheeks still glowing with happiness.

By the time everyone had retired to bed, the rain had arrived as a steady downpour that looked like continuing for some time. It was several days before it eventually gave way to sunshine once more. By that time, tempers were wearing thin. The dampness had even permeated into the farmhouse as dripping coats and boots cluttered the area in front of the kitchen range. It seemed that as soon as one coat dried it was replaced with another wet one. Mel's back ached from her efforts to keep the kitchen's flagstones clean of muddy footprints. It was hard to believe that it was still summer. But at last it stopped, and as if to compensate for all this misery, the sun shone hotter than ever. Windows were thrown open and damp mats spread over the bushes to dry out. At the first possible moment, Mel took the opportunity to slip out to her favourite place—the herb garden. As she walked along the paths, brushing the bushes with her skirts and fingers, she relished the various pungent smells that wafted around her. So different from the cloying scents of other flowers. These scents weren't shy and retiring. They were strong and exciting, each one so different and yet each one demanding to be recognised and acknowledged. She loved them. They didn't have any blowsy colours to catch your attention, and yet they instantly made you aware of their presence. Mel loved to spend time amongst them. She never got tired of working with them, creating pungent oils and salves that had so many uses. She hoped Ruth would create a herb garden when they moved into Hollowtree Cottage. She sighed. It must be wonderful to set up home with the man you love. The image of Josh flashed unbidden into her mind, but she quickly pushed it away, telling herself not to be so stupid. It was no use dreaming of the impossible.

'Mel?' Startled, she turned round. It was as if by thinking of him she had conjured up the man, for Josh was there, standing in front of her. She tried to gather her scattered thoughts. 'Are you alright?' he asked. 'I didn't mean to alarm you. I thought you would have heard me coming.'

'It's OK, I was just wool-gathering. Did you want Aunt Hannah? She's in the house somewhere. Though Ben and my uncle are out across the fields.'

'No, it's you I was looking for. I've come to take you out for your first driving lesson.'

'A driving lesson? I thought you'd decided you wouldn't be seen dead in the dog cart, so what's changed your mind?'

'I haven't changed my mind about the dog cart, but I've brought the gig for you to have a go with.'

Mel stared in horror. 'You mean one of those high spindly things drawn by at least two horses.'

Josh laughed. 'No, I wouldn't be foolish enough to let you loose on one of those on your first lesson. What you probably don't realise is that there are various types of gigs. The one I have waiting outside for you is a smaller version drawn by only one horse. I thought it would be a compromise. Are you up to the challenge?'

'In that case, yes, I'll give it a go. I'll just get my bonnet and shawl.'

'Don't be long, I don't like keeping my horse standing around too long,' he called after her.

* * *

First, Josh brought Mel up to the horse's head.

'Come and say hello to Leah, Mel. She's very quiet. You'll be safe with her.' She tentatively patted Leah's neck, and wished she could be as confident around horses as everyone else. When Josh assisted her up into the double seat of the gig, she was trembling with nervousness and excitement. Neither of which was helped by Josh taking the seat next to her. She could feel the warmth of his thigh against hers and found it very disturbing. The problem was there was no room to move away.

'I'll get Leah started out on the road and then you can take over. Watch how I handle the reins,' Josh told her. Mel tried to concentrate but her mind kept wandering off to the strength and beauty of his long, slender fingers. She jumped when he suddenly reached over and took one of her hands and placed it with his on the reins.

'That's it. Now put your other hand on the reins. Take your time to get accustomed to them.'

What Mel couldn't get accustomed to was the feel of his hands on hers, and the shivery sensations that were coursing through her body. But when he took his hands away, Leah swerved to the right. Mel panicked and pulled hard to the left. The horse stumbled and the gig swayed dangerously. Josh grabbed back the reins.

'I can't do it,' Mel wailed. 'It's no use, Josh. Take me home.'

'Oh, come on, it's not like you to give up at the first fence. I thought you had more pluck than that. Now, calm down and we'll start again.' When they were once more trotting steadily down the lane, he handed Mel the reins again. 'Now pull gently on the right rein to make Leah go right, and the left to the left. To make her stop, pull them back towards you and shout 'Whoa'. But no sudden jerky movements, OK.'

This time she concentrated very hard on the job at hand and soon found her rhythm. Gaining confidence, she relaxed and began to enjoy the ride. Just as she was wishing it would go on forever, Josh said it was time to turn back for home.

'You've done very well for a first attempt. We'll soon have you taking Leah out on your own. But that will do for now,' he said, turning the gig around and retracing their steps. As Josh was driving Mel's thoughts turned to Connor.

'Did you manage to find out anything about Connor's arrest?' she asked.

'Oh yes, I've got some good news and bad news about that. Your Irish friend has been released.'

'That's good news. I knew he'd soon be proven innocent.'

'Well, the bad news is that he hasn't actually been proven innocent.'

Mel frowned. 'But you said he'd been released.'

'My father managed to get him released simply because there was no concrete evidence to prove him guilty, so he's still under suspicion. It was only on my father's word that they released him at all.'

'But what was he accused of? Surely it must have been some trivial thing that annoyed those in charge, simply because he was always nagging them to treat the navvies fairly.'

'I'm afraid it's more serious than that, Mel. O'Flynn is accused of murder.'

CHAPTER 9

'Murder, no, not Connor!' Mel exclaimed. 'He would never murder anyone.'

'You can't know that. Be realistic, Mel. O'Flynn is a navvy and navvies are rough people. They have to be to do what they do. So you cannot expect them to behave like us. What about the day I found him so-called helping you up? He may well have gone on to assault you if I hadn't suddenly appeared.

'No, he really was helping me up,' Mel insisted. 'He wouldn't have hurt me. I just know he's a good man. Papa always said I have a knack for knowing immediately if a person is good or bad. It's because of being brought up amongst business people, I suppose. You can't say because he's a navvy that he's bound to be bad. Rough, maybe, but there must be many good men amongst them as in any other walk of life. Anyway, Connor was already in prison when Sarah was found, so he couldn't have done it.'

'Unfortunately, there have been other cases of girls being assaulted lately, including one murder, and always following the canal's route. However, they have been unable to find any hard evidence against O'Flynn, which is why my father managed to get him released. Though they say he is still under suspicion,' Josh warned.

'He must have been framed,' Mel replied hotly. 'We'll just have to find the real culprit.'

'Now don't you go and do anything foolish. Leave it to the authorities.'

'But if they believe it's Connor, they won't be looking for anyone else. Where is he now? Is he back at work?'

'He's back at their shanty town, but he's not fit for work yet. They treated him pretty rough in prison.'

Mel frowned. 'The poor man, I must go and see him, take him some salves and tinctures.'

'Now don't you go venturing into that shanty town on your own,' Josh said sternly. 'You don't know what might happen. I'm sure they are quite capable of looking after their own without your help.'

'They were glad of our help when they had that landslide, so why wouldn't they welcome our help now? I have to see him. I'll walk over in the morning. It'll be fine, you'll see.'

Josh shook his head. 'I can see it isn't a bit of good forbidding it. So I'll take you. I'll pick you up in the gig after breakfast, alright?'

Mel rewarded him with a beaming smile.

The rest of the drive was made in silence, each deep in their own thoughts. Josh looked grim and Mel chewed her lip anxiously, wondering what she would find in the morning, and trying to decide what salves she should take, not knowing the actual nature of his injuries.

* * *

The following morning, Mel was in the still room before breakfast, packing her basket with salves and herbs that she thought she might need for Connor's injuries. When Josh called for her directly after they'd eaten, she was ready. It was a beautiful, sunny day, with only a handful of puffy clouds scattered across the blue sky. Every tree seemed to vibrate with birdsong. Mel was content to leave the driving to Josh while she revelled in the warmth of the sun on her back. She remembered her first week here. It seemed incredible that she had actually been scared of these wide-open spaces. Now she felt so at home here she couldn't imagine living in a city again. Mel realised with a bit of a shock how much she'd changed since that first day. She felt more alive, taking more interest in the world as a whole. A world she hadn't even known existed. Suddenly she felt all the anger and resentment she had harboured against her father for deserting her, slip away. Now she felt able to grieve for him as she should.

Soon the noise of the canal workings reached them. Just an indistinct rumble at first, getting louder as they advanced until the noise was so intense that it blotted out the sounds of the birdsong completely. Now they could distinguish the individual noises. The thump of the pickaxes on the hard earth; the rumble of the resulting rubble being shovelled into the barrows; the squeak of the wooden wheels as the men pushed them up the steep, narrow planks to be loaded into the carts; the jingle of the horses' harness as they took the loads away; and above it all, the shouts and calls of the myriad of men working there. Mel wondered how the men could stand the continual deafening noise.

'If you are working with it every day you get used to it,' Josh told her.

She was glad when they'd rounded the head and were

travelling down the other side. As they were nearing the shanty town, a big man stepped out in front of them and made a grab at the horse's bridle.

'We don't need the likes of you poking around our town. If you don't want trouble, just turn around and git gone,' he said.

Mel shivered, glad now she hadn't come alone, for he looked very threatening as he stood there with his legs apart, shirt sleeves rolled up to display muscular, weather-tanned forearms. His britches were tied round his middle with a piece of rope, like a flour sack.

'We've not come to cause trouble. Miss Meredith has brought some salves for O'Flynn's injuries,' Josh explained. 'Miss Meredith is from the farm where your injured people were taken after the landslide. She tended to their injuries then.'

'Oh, sorry, I didn't recognise you, Miss. You did a good job then. Me mate reckons he would have died if you hadn't tended to him. O'Flynn lodges with Mrs Price.' The man waved his hand in the direction of the town. 'Her hut's down there on the right. Anyone will tell you.' He stood back and they continued down between the rows of wooden huts, no more than glorified sheds. Mel looked around in astonishment. Were these huts actually people's homes? Some were even just canvas tents. The strip of ground between the rows was just bare earth, long ago denuded of any greenery. A group of half-naked children played in the dirt, watched by a couple of women sitting on the wooden steps of what Mel presumed was their home, each with a young baby held within their shawls. Several other women were about, doing various tasks such as carrying water buckets and spreading the washing to dry. Everywhere shrieked poverty, yet somehow you knew these people were fierce survivors. Hostile stares focused on the fine horse and gig that had unexpectedly arrived among them. Josh jumped down and held the horse's head.

'We are looking for Connor O'Flynn; we were told he is lodging with Mrs Price. Could you direct us to her?'

'Third hut down,' one of the mothers said, nodding in that direction.

One of the children ran up to them. 'I'll show yer, sir. She's me Mam.'

Josh looked around but could find no suitable hitching rail.

'Thanks. And would one of you other boys like to earn a penny looking after my horse', he asked. There was a stampede of little feet and a chorus of 'Me! Me!' Josh selected the most sensible-looking one and handed him the reins. 'She'll be no bother as long as you don't do anything to scare her, OK?' The boy nodded, proudly taking the proffered reins. Josh helped Mel down and turned to Mrs Price's son. 'Right then, lad, lead the way.'

Inside the cramped hut, Connor was lying on one of the four bunk beds, no more than wooden shelves attached to two of the side walls. A table and four chairs took up the rest of the floor space. An iron pot-bellied stove stood in one corner. From the pot sitting on top came an appetizing aroma of what was probably rabbit stew. A glance at the figure struggling to rise from the bed showed Mel how pale Connor was between the horrific cuts and bruises that covered his face and shoulders.

'Oh, Connor,' she exclaimed. 'What have they done to you?'

'Miss Mel, you shouldn't be here. This is no place for you,' Connor told her.

'I've brought some of my salves and poultices to help ease the pain,' she said, ignoring his protests. 'We'll have you fighting fit again in no time.' He sank thankfully back onto the bed. Mrs. Price was hovering over her, wringing her hands.

'I've been doing me best, Miss. I've bathed them bruises regularly in hot water.'

Mel gave the agitated woman a reassuring smile. 'You've done the right thing, Mrs Price. It is very good of you to care for him. Can I trouble you to steep these herbs in a little hot water, while I smooth some of my salves over these bruises? Then we can make up a poultice for his other injuries.'

'Do you have other lodgers as well?' Josh asked, looking around.

'Three.'

He nodded towards the young lad who was hovering wide-eyed in the doorway. 'It can't be easy for you, Mrs Price, having an injured man to care for as well as your own family. It must make a lot of work'.

She looked up from her task with the herbs. 'We take care of our own, sir,' she told him with dignity. 'We may not have much but what we've got we share with any one of us who's in need.'

He looked round at the four bunks, wondering where she and her family slept.

'We have a separate room through there, Sir, for the family,' she told him as if reading his thoughts. 'And the rent from my lodgers means we all eat pretty well.'

When Mel had finished smothering her salves over Connor's bruises, she mixed the herbs Mrs Price had steeped with some honey and spread it onto a piece of cloth that she'd brought with her. Then she placed it gently on the worst of the invalid's injuries.

'There, that's the best I can do for you for now, but it should help the healing. I'll leave you the rest of this salve to use on his bruises tomorrow, if that's alright, Mrs Price.' Mel told the woman as she packed her things away. 'Now, tell us why you were arrested in the first place,' she asked Connor.

'And what's all this nonsense about you having committed a murder?'

'There's not much I can tell you, Miss Mel. These men turned up one evening when they knew I'd be here, and carted me off to Gloucester jail. Said they had proof that I was the one who'd been assaulting village girls and even murdered one. I tried to tell them I was innocent but they wouldn't listen; they just knocked me about and said it was what scum like me deserved.'

Mel flinched, remembering how Josh had called Connor 'scum'. But when she looked at him, it appeared that he had forgotten that.

Josh shook his head. 'But they hadn't any proof, had they? Nothing they produced when my father challenged them counted as proof, just hearsay. That was how we managed to get you freed,' he explained.

'None of it had a gain of truth in it. I was set up.'

'But who would do such a thing? Mel asked.

'I have my suspicions, but, like them, I can't prove it. So it's best I keep mum.'

Mel was horrified to think whoever did this was going to get off scot-free. 'Can't you challenge the person; get the authorities to investigate him or something?'

'You forget, Miss Mel, I'm just an Irish navvy. No one's going to take my word against those in high places. I'd just lose my job and then I wouldn't be able to help anyone.'

Josh frowned. 'Are you implying that it isn't a navvy who is committing these acts?'

Connor shook his head. 'No, I'm not saying that. In fact, I believe that it probably was a navvy. I'm saying it wasn't a navvy that had me thrown into prison. I think that was for a completely different reason. I think that by continuing to push for better conditions for the workers, I was treading on someone's toes. They found an easy way to put a stop to it.'

'These are serious accusations you're making, O'Flynn. You could get into a lot of trouble if you broadcast it,' Josh warned.

'I know, but if their game isn't stopped, things could get very nasty. As it is the navvies are getting restless. Their wages keep getting docked with excuses that they've either lost or broken various pieces of equipment. As soon as I'm fit for work again I shall continue to investigate.'

'Oh, please be careful, Connor,' Mel pleaded. 'Next time could be worse for you. Josh, couldn't you look into things? Your father is on the canal's trustee committee.'

'I'll see what I can do, but I'm not making any promises,' Josh told them. 'Now I really must get you home Mel, or your aunt will worry.' He threw a handful of coins onto the table. 'Something to help towards Connor's keep, as I don't suppose he's able to pay his rent while he's not working.'

Mrs Price looked as though she was going to refuse, then she looked at Connor, and smiled her acceptance.

'Thank you, sir. I'll take good care of him.'

With a reassuring smile to Connor, Mel gathered her things and they left the hut. Outside, the boy in charge of Josh's horse was still standing stiffly at its head, hanging on to the reins so tight his fingers had turned white.

'Any trouble with her?' Josh asked.

The boy shook his head so fiercely that his unruly thatch of hair looked as though it would take off. Josh handed the lad two pennies, causing his eyes to widen before he dashed off to show his mother. Chuckling to himself, Josh handed Mel up into the gig and they were homeward bound. As they passed through the settlement, Mel looked around.

'Is it me, or do you feel a certain tension in the air? She asked Josh.

He nodded. 'You're right. It's almost as if they are waiting for something to happen. What's the betting that 'something' will be trouble? If the workers are really having their wages docked unnecessarily, I think I should look into it. It's categorically only Rupert Johnson's responsibility, and has nothing to do with me. But, even at the risk of upsetting Johnson, I think it should be investigated. This canal is costing more than was estimated anyway, without more stoppages and disruptions. My father has a lot invested in this venture.' As Mel frowned, Josh looked closely at her. She looked so lovely, so refreshingly innocent, that it made Josh realise he'd been speaking as though she was another man and not a delicately brought up young lady. Trouble was, she had such a down-to-earth approach to life that he often forgot these things weren't for young ladies' ears. 'I'm sorry, Miss Meredith, I was thinking aloud.'

Mel looked at him in surprise. 'Why so formal all of a sudden? I thought we'd agreed you would call me Mel? I'm not offended that you're talking with me about these things. I'm interested. You know that!'

'I forget sometimes that you are a gentle-born lady. This is not a suitable subject I should be discussing with you.'

'What's got into you, Josh? This is Mel you're talking to—the girl who was brought up in 'trade' remember, not some refined ballroom. You know I've always been interested in the welfare of these workers, and just because there may be trouble brewing doesn't mean I'll change my mind. So tell me, what do you think is about to happen?' Mel demanded.

'I don't know what's going to happen. But I'm certain something is. And I don't want you mixed up in it. So promise me, for your own safety, you'll stay away from here.'

She sighed. 'Alright, I'll promise not to go back there alone, just as long as you promise to stop treating me with kid gloves and we can go back to as we were.'

Josh laughed. 'OK. I promise. Now let's forget the canal's troubles for a while and enjoy this beautiful day.'

They continued the rest of the journey back in companionable silence. Well, except for Mel's many interested questions about the birds they heard and the flowers they passed on the way. As they neared the farm, Mel's thoughts returned to the canal and its problems.

'Do you really think there'll be trouble at the canal site? What sort of trouble? Are they likely to attack the village – or our farm?' Should we warn the people?'

Josh shook his head. 'No, not at this point. We don't know for certain if there is going to be trouble and we may make it worse by getting the villagers worried. They're already suspicious of the navvies as it is. It may only need a simple rumour to set off a whole barrel of fireworks. Let it lie for a bit while I make some discreet enquiries.'

She nodded. 'I wish we had some way of catching the real murderer.'

'Now, don't you go poking your pretty little nose into that business! It could be dangerous. Leave it to the authorities. That's their job.'

'But if they believe it's Connor, they won't be looking for anyone else. Is there no other way of finding out?'

'I'm sure they'll find him in the end. Here we are,' Josh said, pulling the gig to a stop by the farm gate. He jumped down, and, looping the reins over the gatepost, came round to help Mel. With his arms around her waist, he lifted her down. As her feet touched the ground, Mel was aware of how close their bodies were. Josh seemed reluctant to let her go and when she looked up, the expression in his eyes made her heart miss a beat. As he lowered his head she realized he was going to kiss her. She knew she should stop him and turn her head away, but instead she raised her face to meet his.

'You're back. Did you see the lad?' Her uncle's voice made them jump guiltily apart. As John Preston came across the yard, Mel hoped he hadn't seen anything to compromise them. She quickly readjusted her shawl, hoping her uncle would put her rather flushed cheeks down to the fresh air.

'Yes, he's been knocked about a bit,' Josh told him. 'But he's being well cared for over there. However, I think there's more to this than meets the eye. I intend to investigate further.'

'Be careful, and let me know what you find, won't you? Mel asked.

'I will, but don't you worry. Forget about the canal and get on with enjoying life,' he called back as he drove away.

But the canal wasn't going to let anyone forget it.

CHAPTER 10

At the back door, Mel met Rupert Johnson coming out.

'Miss Meredith, been visiting your fellow felon, have you?' His smile was far from welcoming.

She stared at him. 'I don't know what you mean?'

'Oh, don't act the innocent with me. Meredith is not a very common surname. Would a certain Hubert Meredith be your father by any chance?'

Mel merely nodded, wondering what he was on about.

'I've just had a visit from a colleague of mine who's just arrived from Birmingham. He reported a certain scandal concerning your father. You are always putting on airs and graces, making out you're better than others. What will people say when they discover your father is a criminal?'

'My father was the most honest man you could find. He is no criminal.' She stared up at him, her eyes sparking outrage. 'I demand you take back those filthy lies.'

He laughed. 'Make sure of your facts before you get on your high horse, young lady. Don't you agree that it's against the law to take a life?'

'Of course, but. . . .'

'That includes taking your own life. Your father committed the crime of suicide. That's why you arrived with only the clothes on your back. In these situations, the Crown confiscates all the man's possessions as punishment.'

Mel could feel a scream bubbling up inside her, but she forced it back. She wouldn't give this horrid man the satisfaction of seeing her break down. Gritting her teeth, she threw back her head and stared defiantly straight into his eyes.

'It doesn't matter what he had done previously. Now he will be forever branded as a criminal.' Rupert continued, rubbing it in. 'No wonder you feel sympathy with that Irish crook.' Then, with a smug smile on his face, he walked away.

Mel stood there, unable to move or even think as her world crashed down around her ears. Then she turned and fled to the familiarity of her herb garden. There, with tears running down her cheeks, she sank to her knees between the fragrant rows of herbs and was sick. Why had no one told her the truth? She thought her father's things had been sold to pay off debts.

'Oh Papa, how could you? Didn't you give any thought to me? I thought you loved me.'

It was bad enough that the business was gone when she had expected to inherit it. She had such dreams of carrying it on in her father's footsteps. But to suddenly learn that her father was labelled a criminal? She would never lift up her head again. Eventually, she went indoors. Her aunt took one worried look at her and, tactfully asking no questions, bundled her up to bed with one of her tinctures.

That night, Mel tossed and turned in her narrow bed under the eaves. She had started to feel as though she belonged here. That people liked and respected her. What would they say when the truth of her past came out? Would she be able to keep it a secret? And what of Josh? She was sure he had been about to kiss her before her uncle arrived. The promise of it had sent a warm shiver of anticipation through her. She had realised that this was what she'd always been wishing for. Her heart began to race just at the thought of his lips claiming hers. Now she knew she must never allow it. As much as she may long for it, there could be no happy ending for her. If it had just been the fact that her family had been in trade and Josh's father was a lord, they might still have resolved things, but this terrible secret of hers would always be a barrier between them. A secret Josh must never even guess at. She couldn't bear to lose his friendship or his support in her fight for justice for Connor. So she must be forever on her guard and never allow any moments like yesterday to be repeated.

The next morning at breakfast, her aunt commented on her wan looks.

'Didn't you sleep well, dear?' she asked. 'You mustn't worry about that young navvy. I'm sure he'll make a full recovery.'

Mel felt bad for allowing her aunt to believe this was what had disturbed her sleep. What made her feel worse was when she realised she had been so taken up by the discovery of her dreadful secret and her feelings for Josh, that she'd hardly given Connor a thought. She told herself she must stop it. Rupert Johnson looked up from his breakfast.

'We'd all sleep better if that villain was still in prison,' he said sourly.

'How can you say that? He's innocent,' Mel retorted hotly.

The engineer glared back at her.

'You can't prove that? You're like all the other stupid village girls – taken in by his so-called Irish charm. You'll be crying a very different tune if you're not careful.'

'Now then, Mr. Johnson, there's no need to talk to my niece like that.' Her aunt told him firmly.

'I'm just saying, now he's free, there'll be trouble. You wait and see.'

He stood up, crashing back his chair, and with a final glare in her direction, he slammed out of the room. Everyone just looked at each other in amazement. But Mel frowned. The engineer was behaving as though their conversation of the previous day had never happened. While she was glad he'd obviously decided not to broadcast the facts, she still didn't trust him. What game was he playing now? Then her uncle patted her arm.

'Never mind, lass. I've just the thing to cheer you up,' he told her. 'If you've finished your breakfast, come on out with me. I've something to show you.'

'I'd love to, after I've helped Aunt Hannah clear away,' she answered.

'Leave that, my dear. You go on outside. It's a bright, sunny day, and maybe it'll put some roses back in your cheeks.'

Although it was still early, Mel could feel the sun warming her back as she followed her uncle across the yard. As they stopped outside the cow byre, her uncle turned to her.

'Ready lass?' he asked. She nodded and he opened the door.

Mel peered into the gloom of the shed and saw Bluebell, one of their milking cows, contentedly chewing her cud. Just as she was wondering why her uncle had brought her here, she noticed something lying beside her. As the light from the open door fell across it, it struggled to its feet. Mel gasped in delight. It was a baby calf, a perfect miniature of its mother, its hair in tight little curls over its forehead. Big, liquid brown eyes stared up at her.

'Oh, she's gorgeous. Can I stroke her? Is it a she, or a he?'

'If you go quietly, Bluebell won't mind. It's a she, a little heifer, and will make a welcome addition to our herd.' Mel inched her way towards the calf, hand outstretched, making cooing noises. On trembling legs, the little animal gingerly sniffed Mel's hand and then bounded away behind its mother. Mel laughed, asking what her name was.

'She hasn't got one yet.' Her uncle smiled at her obvious delight. 'Perhaps you'd like to name her?'

'Star – because I think she is a star. What d'you think, Uncle John?'

He laughed. 'Then Star she will be. Now we'd best leave them in peace because Bluebell is looking a bit agitated.' Her uncle quietly closed the shed door and went off to deal with the other animals.

Mel wandered across the yard and leaned over the gate, enjoying the warmth of the sun. Sam, the sheepdog, rubbed against her leg and she patted his head.

'You're happy to have me around, aren't you, boy? That's more than I can say of that old gander over there.' She nodded to the other end of the yard, where the bird was staring at her with his cold beady eyes. He knew to keep his distance with Sam around. In the end, grumbling to himself, he led his ladies off to the pond. He reminded Mel of Rupert Johnson and she laughed at the comparison. But then frowned as she wondered at the engineer's antagonism that seemed to be directed towards her. Was it just because she'd helped Connor? Or did it stem from when she'd mentioned looking over his account books? She looked out across the fields at the canal workings in the distance. It should have been a straightforward job, driving a canal across a few fields from Gloucester to Berkley. It certainly made sense for the ships to bypass that treacherous strip of the Severn. Although, she was sure those who planned it never anticipated the effect it would have on the people both involved with its building and those who lived adjacent to it. But then again, did they really care? Her own experience should have answered that. The thought saddened her. Then she suddenly became aware of the sweet trilling notes of a birdsong, but where was the bird? She could hear it, but couldn't locate it. Then, looking up to the sky she saw it; just a dot with fluttering wings, hovering high above the fields, singing so sweetly and so strongly. How could this tiny bird put so much energy into singing whilst hovering so high above her? Listening to the pure joy of that song, Mel found herself relaxing. Now calm, she retraced her steps to the farmhouse so that she could begin that morning's chores.

As it was a lovely sunny day, Hannah decided to give the bedrooms a good spring clean. Mel helped her strip the beds and bring the blankets, pillows and rugs outside to give them a good shake. They were spread over the bushes for a couple of hours to air them, while Hannah and Mel swept the floors, dusted and polished the furniture and floorboards, and cleaned the windows. Then everything had to be taken back upstairs and reinstated. By bedtime, Mel was exhausted and slept soundly all night.

Mel was pleased when Josh turned up the next day and offered to take her back to the navvies' village to see how her patient was getting on. She quickly collected more salve and tincture in case of any headaches, then she was ready. The weather was still sunny and she enjoyed bowling along in the gig beside Josh. He even let her take the reins again until they got nearer the canal workings, and the noise made the horse restless. She was glad to hand them back to Josh then. This time their arrival wasn't met with any hostility, and they drove straight through without any trouble. Connor was sitting on a bench outside the hut and rose to welcome them. The same young lad dashed forward and offered to hold the horse again. No doubt remembering the tuppence Josh had given him last time . . .

'Glad to see you up and about, O'Flynn,' Josh greeted him.

Connor grinned. 'Yes, thanks to Miss Mel's salves. They've worked wonders. I shall be back at work tomorrow.'

'You're certainly looking better. I've brought some more in case you need them,' Mel said, pleased to see the mischievous glint back in his eyes.

'Thank you Miss Mel. Have you found out anything, Sir?' Connor asked.

'No, not yet, but I haven't given up. How about you? Any news at all?'

Connor shook his head. 'No, but once I'm back at work I'm expecting to pick up some clues. I hope so, anyway. It's unsettling still having this hanging over my head. They just don't want to believe I'm innocent.'

'Don't lose heart. Something will turn up,' Josh reassured him. 'But we must be away now. I have an appointment.'

'It's good of you both to come. Thank you, and may we get some results soon.'

Rewarding the horse attendant with another two pennies, they were on their way. Once they were underway, Mel asked if Josh thought there was any chance of finding the culprit.

Josh frowned. 'There's always the chance. It's possible he may strike again and maybe leave some clues. But I think your friend is right in thinking that his arrest was nothing to do with the attacks on these women, but a different reason altogether. And that reason I find more pressing because it seems to point to someone with authority within this canal-building project. We don't know if it's merely aimed at stopping the canal building or at something that could endanger the lives of all the workers.'

The rest of the journey was spent in silence, with both of them deep in thought.

The following day was Sunday, and a special day for Ben and Ruth because their bans were to be read out. The hot weather was continuing so to boost her morale, Mel decided to wear her new green dress that she and her aunt had made from the material they'd bought at the market.

'My, you look very summery.' Hannah teased. 'With your auburn hair, green really suits you.'

'Thank you for helping me make it, aunt. I must admit, I feel good in it. Is that being very vain?'

'Of course not, dear. We want you to feel good and enjoy life again. We can't take away the pain of your past but we can try and make the present better.'

Mel felt the tears welling up in her eyes and she gave her aunt a big hug.

'Oh Aunt Hannah, I don't know what I'd have done if you hadn't wanted me. Instead, you've made me feel like one of the family. I'm so grateful.'

'Get away with you, lass. Now, we must get a move on or we'll be late for church.'

The church was full and as they sat down, Mel whispered to her aunt.

'Ben and Ruth both look so happy, holding hands. You must be glad he's found someone he really loves, Aunt Hannah.'

'Yes, I think they'll do well together. Ruth is a very sensible girl. Then it will be your turn to find someone.'

Mel shook her head. 'I don't think there's much hope of that,' she said sadly, her eyes drawn towards the other side of the church where Josh was sitting with his sister. She knew she didn't dare even hope. Beside him, Fleur was looking very bright and cheerful. She sighed. Mel had hoped she would have seen more of Fleur, even become close friends. But that hadn't happened. In fact, she had been very noticeable in her absence lately. So it came as a surprise when, as they all filed out of the church, the young lady made a beeline for her.

'I'm so glad to see you, Mel,' she said, linking arms with her. 'You see, I've got a secret and I'm bursting to tell someone. As you're my friend, I know you won't tell anyone else, will you?'

Mel sighed. She didn't really want to hear any more secrets.

'Oh Mel,' Fleur continued. 'I'm in love and it's wonderful. I feel like I'm walking on air, and the sun is always shining. Have you ever been in love, Mel?'

Mel laughed. 'Obviously not, if that's how it makes you feel. But who's the lucky man?' She remembered the many occasions she'd glimpsed Fleur with the engineer and prayed that it wasn't him.

'Oh, you don't know him. He lives in the next village – Hatfield Court. Promise you won't tell on me.'

'Of course, but why do you need to keep it a secret?'

'My parents think I'm too young to know my own mind and want me to have a season in London next year. But I just know I won't meet anyone else that makes me feel like this. It's so frustrating not being able to tell everyone. That's why I had to tell you. You do understand, don't you?'

'I'm glad to see you so happy, Fleur, and I really hope it works out for you. But you'll have to tell your family sometime. What about Josh? Couldn't you confide in him? He may help you persuade your parents.'

'Oh no, Josh is stricter than my father about who I meet. You won't tell him, will you?'

'No. I won't tell a soul,' Mel assured her, as Josh called Fleur to get on the coach with the rest of the family. With a cheerful wave, she skipped off to join them.

Ruth and the vicar had been invited back to the farm for a meal. Hannah had served up a saddle of mutton stuffed with parsley, thyme, onions and hard-boiled eggs, and a rabbit pie. A feast to tempt anyone. But Mel had no appetite, and only picked at her food. Across the table from her, Ben and Ruth, hands and eyes constantly meeting, were oblivious to all except each other. Their love just emphasised her own lonely future. With an ache deep in her heart, she knew this would never be possible for her, not with her terrible secret.

Her aunt frowned. 'You've hardly eaten anything, Mel. Are you not well?'

'I'm alright, it's just the heat. Do you mind if I go outside for a while, Aunt Hannah?'

'Ay, it's very sticky, isn't it? I reckon there's a storm in the offing, so don't go far,' her uncle warned.

Glad to be out on her own, Mel struck out across the fields. All this talk of love and weddings had made her depressed. She realized that this would never be her destiny now. Josh's handsome face came to mind; the way his eyes changed from summer skies to chips of blue ice, depending on his mood, and how she itched to push back his corn-coloured hair when it kept flopping over his eyes. She remembered how her heartbeat increased when they very nearly kissed. She had never felt like this before. Certainly, her previous experience with romance—before the viscount had broken off their engagement following the death of her father—hadn't made her feel like this. She'd vowed then never to trust her heart to another. Now she could see the wisdom of this. She must make sure she kept Josh at arms-length, whatever the cost.

Fat plops of rain on her cotton-clad shoulders brought her back to her surroundings, and she became aware of the rumble of thunder in the distance. Mel had never grown out of being scared of thunder. It was time to turn back. But before she'd gone far, the storm broke. She was drenched in seconds. Then the thunder crashed around her. She dived into a nearby barn and curled up in the corner, burying herself under a pile of straw. Tears streaked down her face and she trembled with cold and fear. When someone touched her shoulder she screamed with fright. Was she to be the next person to be accosted and probably murdered? Was the accursed canal about to claim yet another victim?

CHAPTER 11

Mel's body tensed in trepidation. Was it Josh? But why didn't he say something? She tried to turn round but the hand moved to the small of her back and pushed her face hard into the straw. Struggling to breathe, she managed to twist her head slightly sideways until she could suck some air into her tortured lungs. Then she felt his other hand, calloused and work-roughened, sliding under her skirts and up her leg. This wasn't Josh. This could only be the villain they'd been trying to catch. But now he'd caught her. Mel's eyes closed; every muscle in her body tensed in trepidation and fear. She began to shake. Never before had she felt so violated, so vulnerable. All her energy melted away, leaving her weak and helpless. This was it. She was about to die. No, her brain screamed. She wouldn't let this happen. She forced her body into action again, kicking her legs, trying to draw up her knee. But he was too strong for her. His fingers dug into her leg muscles and she yelped with the pain. She heard him laugh—an evil laugh that shocked her. But it also strengthened her determination to escape him. Her hands clutched at the straw, trying to find leverage to drag herself out of reach. But the straw just gave way. Desperately she stretched out further until her fingers touched wood—a thick stick of some sort, probably a broken fork handle. Then, as hard as she could, she swung it out behind her. Her shoulder jarred painfully as it made contact. With a grunt, a body slumped down on top of her. The stench of body odour and sour ale threatened to overwhelm her, and she had to swallow hard to stop herself from being sick. Quickly she wriggled out from under him, making for the door. Just in time, as the man, recovering his senses, grunted and lunged for her, catching the hem of her dress. She wrenched it away from him, not caring when she heard it rip. Gathering the bulk of it about her waist, she bolted out of the barn into the torrential rain. Thunder still crashed overhead. But the fear of what was behind her was greater than her fear of thunder, and she raced on, blood pounding in her ears and brain. Blinded by rain and tears, she prayed that she was heading in the right direction. Then a man's arms were holding her tightly and she screamed, slipping into a black void.

When Mel next opened her eyes she was in her own bed. Her aunt and uncle were dozing in chairs beside her. She blinked, trying to work out why she was in bed when her window clearly showed it was daytime. It was that laugh she remembered first. Then the roughness of a hand sliding up her leg. She shuddered. Dreams were supposed to fade away when you woke up, but this one persisted. More of a nightmare than a dream. And why were her aunt and uncle here? Had she screamed out in her sleep?

'She's awake, Hannah.' Her uncle shook his wife. Mel looked at him, puzzled. He should be outside, seeing to the animals. Her aunt jumped up, laying her hand on Mel's forehead.

'Oh, thank goodness you're back with us. How d'you feel, my dear?'

'Why am I in bed in the daytime? What has happened?'

'Don't you remember?' her aunt asked. 'You fainted. When your uncle saw you running across the field in the rain, he went to meet you. But then you collapsed in his arms and lost consciousness. He carried you up here and I got you out of your wet clothes and put you to bed. But when you still didn't regain consciousness we were worried. It was obvious it was not just the storm that frightened you, but we didn't know what. Can you manage to tell us?'

Slowly, images came back to Mel. She tried to push them back into the recesses of her mind but they wouldn't go. She realized then that she hadn't been dreaming. The nightmare was real. Shudders ripped through her body as she become aware of how lucky she'd been to escape with her life. Tears streamed down her cheeks unchecked.

'Oh, you poor dear.' Her aunt gathered her in her arms. 'It's alright. Nothing is going to hurt you now.' She held Mel, rocking her gently until the shaking stopped and she could wipe away the tears. 'There now, you settle back down and I'll fetch you a tincture to help you sleep. You'll feel better in the morning. We'll talk then. She ushered her husband out of the door.

Despite her aunt's tincture, Mel had a restless night, haunted by hands reaching out for her, no matter in which direction she ran.

In the morning she woke with a sore throat and a raging fever, no doubt brought on by shock and the soaking she'd received running through the storm. For over a week she was barely aware of her aunt and Ruth bathing her burning body with cold water and cooling poultices, pressing her to take constant sips of water. At last, the fever broke, and she began the slow road back to health. She was still very weak, but at least she could now receive visitors. Her first one was Ruth.

'I'm pleased to see you're on the mend, Mel. We were very

worried about you. I've brought you some flowers to cheer you up,' she told her, putting a vase of large white daisies on the bedside table.

'Thank you, Ruth, they're lovely. What are they called?'

'They are known locally as moon-daisies. They grow wild in the hay meadows at this time of year. I mustn't stay long as we don't want to tire you, but I need you to help me with my wedding trousseau.'

'How's it coming along?'

'All quite smoothly so far, but, as I haven't any sisters to turn to I would value your advice.'

Mel gave a rather croaky laugh. 'I can't claim to be an expert on weddings. I've never even been to one, especially not a country wedding,' she warned. 'But it will be lovely to be back and useful again. I feel I've been such a burden, giving Aunt Hannah so much work on top of her usual chores. If only I didn't feel so weak.'

'You couldn't help getting sick, and your aunt loves having you here, so she wouldn't mind. Anyway, I gave her a hand whenever I could. You're bound to feel weak for a bit. The secret is not to try and do too much before your body is ready, or you could be back where you started.'

'Now, don't you go tiring her out.' Her aunt, coming in with another of her special tonics, told Ruth.

'No, I'm just off. Get well quickly, won't you, Mel,' Ruth said as she left the room.

'How are you feeling, pet?' her aunt asked, placing a cool hand on Mel's forehead. 'Your temperature seems to have gone down anyway.'

'I'm much better, Aunt Hannah. Just looking forward to coming downstairs. It's a long haul for you, having to keep coming up here.'

'Don't you bother your head about that, my girl. You just concentrate on getting your strength back. You've had several visitors asking after you, especially Josh Benchard. He's been most persistent.'

Mel's heart missed a beat at the thought of Josh being eager to see her. But then common sense told her he was merely keen to know if she could tell him anything that would help track down this villain that was terrorising the neighbourhood. Well, she very much doubted she'd be much help there.

'But now, my dear,' her aunt continued, 'we must talk about the time of the storm. I know it must be painful to think of it, but we need to know exactly what happened. It wasn't just the thunder that upset you, was it?'

Mel shuddered. She didn't want to go there, even though she knew she must.

'It was sunny when I started out for that walk. Then the storm came in very rapidly—not only the rain but thunder as well. I have always been petrified of thunder so I ran into the barn and flung myself face down onto the straw. I didn't realise there was anyone else in there until they touched my shoulder. At first, I thought it was Josh or Connor, and I tried to turn around. But I knew it wasn't because when he pushed me back into the straw, he smelt awful. That was when I guessed it must be the killer we've been searching for, and that I might be murdered. Luckily I found a bit of wood and I swung it hard behind me. It must have caught him on the side of his head because he slumped down on top of me. I managed to wriggle out and get away just as he came to. Then I ran. Even the thunder didn't seem as frightening as that man. But when I felt someone's arms catch me, I thought it was him and that was all I remember. The next thing I knew, I was up here in bed.' Mel was shaking badly by the time she recounted her ordeal, and she buried her face in her hands.

'So he didn't hurt you any more than that?' her aunt persisted, relief evident in her voice.

Mel shook her head.

'It was your Uncle John who caught you in his arms. He saw you racing across the field as though Samson our big black bull, was at your heels, and went to meet you. You frightened him when you screamed and fainted. He hadn't been expecting that sort of reaction. He was nearly as white as you when he carried you in, poor man. I thought I was about to have two invalids on my hands.' This brought a shaky smile from Mel, just as Hannah hoped. 'Now you settle back down and try and sleep. That's what is going to get you better and on your feet again.'

Feeling emotionally drained, Mel's eyes were already closing. Hannah gently tucked her in, kissed her forehead, and left the room.

It was several more days before Mel felt strong enough to come downstairs. As the weather had turned warm again, she was sitting in her favourite spot in the herb garden when Josh called. Her heart gave an excited skip when she saw his tall, aristocratic figure striding towards her through the herbs. His smile warming her more than the sun above.

'It's good to see you up and about again, Mel. How are you feeling?' he asked.

'Getting my strength back slowly,' she told him. 'You heard what happened?'

'Yes. Thank goodness it wasn't worse.'

'You think it was the same man that attacked the others?'

'I'm pretty certain it was. If only we could pin him down, but we've still got no leads at all.' Mel frowned. 'If only I'd got a better look at him. But all I could think of was getting away.'

'It was the right thing to do. If you'd hesitated and tried to see him better, it may have been a completely different story. But it proves he's still active in the area. He must be caught before there's another tragedy. I am going to look into the possibility of engaging the help of the Bow Street Runners from London.'

'I think I've heard of them. Weren't they known as Thief-takers?' she asked.

'That was how they started, but they are more official now. I just hope they will consider it worth their while coming out this far. Maybe my father, as the local magistrate, can add a bit of weight. In the meantime, promise me you won't go wandering off on your own.'

She shuddered. 'Don't worry; I've learnt my lesson in that direction.'

'If we do persuade one of these Runners to investigate, they'll want to interview you. You'll have to go over it all again in detail. It won't be pleasant. Would you be up to it, Mel?'

'I know it will be hard, but if it leads to this villain being caught, I'll do whatever they want,' she told him firmly.

Josh smiled. 'I knew you'd do the right thing. You're a brave girl. Now, to change the subject, would you like to go for a drive tomorrow?'

'That would be lovely, Josh. I'm fed up with looking at four walls. Can we continue my driving lesson?'

He shook his head. 'Not this time, Mel. You're not strong enough yet and I wouldn't like the horse to bolt with you. But once you've fully recovered, I promise we'll continue them. Now I must be away. I'll pick you up at two tomorrow. Wrap up warm even though the weather is good—I don't want you to have a relapse.' Then he was gone.

Mel felt like singing. Josh thought she was brave and he was going to take her out tomorrow.

'Oh crazy heart, stop dreaming impossible dreams. You know he can never be yours,' she murmured, running her hand through the aromatic herbs, inhaling their comforting scent.

Mel woke the next morning feeling better than she had for a long time. At last, she seemed to have shaken off the illness that had struck her down. Jumping quickly out of bed, she used the water from the jug on her washstand, shuddering at the cold water on her face and hands. But nothing was going to depress her today. The sun was shining, promising another warm day, and Josh was taking her for a drive this afternoon. Her aunt looked up in surprise as she skipped down the stairs.

'It's good to see you looking so much better, dear,' she said. 'You've actually got some colour in your cheeks again. Sit down and get this breakfast down you. What are you doing today?'

'This morning, I'm helping Ruth with the finishing touches to our dresses and doing other things for the wedding. Then Josh is taking me for a drive this afternoon.'

'Are you sure you're well enough, dear?'

'Oh yes, Aunt Hannah,' Mel said quickly before she could forbid it. 'I'll wrap up warm. The fresh air will do me good.' As well as being close to Josh, she added mentally. Just the thought of him gave her a warm glow, but she knew she was being stupid—with her secret, that way of thinking could only lead to heartache. Josh Benchard was not for her. It seemed that a black cloud had suddenly passed over the sun.

Mel and Ruth spent a busy morning sorting out the details of the wedding. The men had cleared out the barn and brought out the trestle tables and benches usually used for the harvest supper and dance held later on in the year. Now that the big day was getting close, Ruth was a mixture of excitement and nerves, constantly asking Mel questions like 'Will it be alright?', 'Am I doing the right thing in marrying Ben?', Does he really love me?', 'What if I disappointed him?', 'I'm not as good a cook as his mother, what if Hannah thinks Ben has made the wrong choice?', and 'What if it rains on the day?'

Mel laughingly reassured her, reminding her that every bride must have the same fears. It was stepping out into the unknown, but as long as they loved each other, it would all work out in the end. The trouble was, she knew there could be no happy ending for her. She had fallen for the wrong man. If he had been someone like Ben, her secret probably wouldn't make much difference. But to someone of Josh's standing, it would be unthinkable.

Nevertheless, when Josh was handing Mel up into his gig at two o'clock, she couldn't prevent her heart from racing at his touch or the warm glow that she felt as he climbed up beside her. She pulled her shawl tighter round her shoulders, the soft green ribbons on her jaunty straw bonnet matching it.

'I thought we'd take the lanes away from the canal today for a change,' Josh told her when she asked where they were going. 'We'll forget about the canal and its troubles for a few hours.'

Mel was happy with this and, pushing all her other worries aside, settled down to enjoy the scenery. After all, it was a beautiful day, the sun was shining, the birds were singing and Josh was beside her. What more could she ask for? Her spirits soared. Looking around for the bird whose song seemed to fill the whole area, she could just make out a small speck high up in the sky.

'Surely that's not the bird we can hear singing?' Mel asked, pointing skywards.

'Yes, that's a skylark.' Josh told her. 'Whereas most birds perch somewhere to sing, the skylark likes to sing on the wing. To me, the song of the skylark epitomises summer.'

'It's a very unforgettable song. I've heard it sing before but didn't know its name. I'm trying to identify the birds, but so far I've only learnt the robin that is always at my feet when I'm weeding the herb garden and the many sparrows that scratch around the yard when we've fed the hens.' Mel sighed. 'There's so much I don't know.'

Josh laughed. 'At least you're learning. You can't expect to know it all at once. You've only lived in the country a few months.'

Mel was surprised. 'Yes, it is only months. It feels as though I've been here for years.'

'That's not surprising. You seem to have had a very eventful few months. Do you miss the city?'

'No. I miss my father, but that is all.' Her sunny mood evaporated as she thought of her father. Then, determinedly pushing those thoughts away, she turned again to the scenery around them. 'I've never seen so many wildflowers growing amongst the grass. Every field is awash with them.'

'Not for much longer. In a couple of weeks, these fields will all be cut for hay.'

'Oh yes, I remember Ruth saying they wanted to get married before the haymaking. I do hope it all works out well for them.'

'I'm sure it will. You can't take everyone's problems on your shoulders, so stop worrying. Just enjoy today. Leave tomorrow to take care of itself,' Josh told her with a laugh.

She gave him a rueful grin. After all, there was no reason for anything to go wrong. And she still had the rest of the afternoon with Josh to enjoy.

CHAPTER 12

With the wedding only two days away, Mel was roped in to help her aunt with the cooking and baking. As Ruth's father was a widower, Hannah had suggested that the wedding breakfast would be held at the farm. A suggestion that the vicar gratefully accepted.

'We must bring the salted ham up from the cellar to boil, and roast a large joint of beef. There is also some brawn in those earthenware dishes, from when we killed the pig. I wonder if I should ask John to kill a goose as well?' Hannah said, running through the list of things they needed to do.

'I'd certainly be happy if you wrung the neck of that hateful gander, Aunt Hannah. I swear he lies in wait for me.'

Her aunt laughed. 'No doubt, but it wouldn't be him we'd kill. Not only does he make a very good watchdog, but also, none of his wives would produce goslings without him. Maybe we won't want a goose anyway, if we have a few rabbit and pigeon pies, and cheeses and loaves of bread with my homemade pickles and chutneys. Then there'll be fruit tarts, custards and creams.'

'Goodness, Aunt Hannah, how many guests are coming to this wedding?'

'Ah, well lass, everyone likes a wedding and, being one of the richer yeoman farmers in the area, folks expect it of us. So pop out to the garden and see what ripe soft fruits you can find, there's a good girl.'

It was while she was out amongst the fruit bushes that her aunt called out that she had some visitors. Straightening up, she saw Josh and another man coming across the garden towards her.

'Hello, Mel, I've brought Mr Browning to see you. Mr Browning is from the Bow Street Runners,' Josh explained. 'He'd like to get your first-hand account of what happened to you the other day. I hope that's alright.'

'Oh, yes, I suppose.' Mel shuddered. She didn't want to be reminded of the ordeal, much less go over it in detail with this stranger. He wasn't even the sort of man that inspired confidence. Rather a man that one could easily overlook. Looking at his brown broadcloth coat, his mousy brown hair, and his sallow complexion, she thought it was a case of brown by name and brown by nature. But no doubt it was probably an advantage to be nondescript in his line of work.

'Perhaps you'd prefer to sit indoors, Miss Meredith?' he asked, surprisingly gently.

'No.' Mel mentally shook herself. She had to do this if they were to have any hope of catching this villain. 'Would you mind if we sat outside? There's a bench in the herb garden.'

'Yes, that will do fine. Lead the way, miss.'

Josh hung back. 'I'll wait by the gate, Mel. We'll talk later.'

On the way, Mel brushed her hand over the fragrant bushes, their familiar pungent scent easing her nerves. As she sat there in her favourite seat next to the detective, she steeled herself to re-live the worst moment of her life. The very first question he asked was: "Did you get a good look at him". Miserably, she shook her head.

'No, I was lying face down on the straw when he came at me. Every time I tried to turn my head he pushed me back. I'm sorry. I know I should have looked at him when I got free, but all I could think of was getting away.'

'Of course. I wouldn't expect anything else. But just think back about small details. Did he give the impression of being a big man – maybe fat or skinny? Did he have an accent?'

'I think he was big – and strong.'

'A manual worker, perhaps?'

'His hands were big and rough. Yes, I think he was definitely a manual worker. And he smelt horrible, as though he hadn't washed much.'

'That's a great help, miss. It narrows the field and helps us eliminate one of our suspects anyway. Anything else?' the bow street runner asked her.

Mel shook her head. 'No, sorry. Oh yes, there was his laugh.' She shuddered. 'It was the evilest laugh I've ever heard. I shall never forget it.'

As the sound of it filled her head, her eyes filled. She bit her lip, trying to hold them back, but her whole body was shaking at the memory.

Mr Browning stood up. 'Thank you, Miss Meredith. You've been a great help. I'm sure we'll soon have him behind bars.'

As he walked away, Josh came forward and sat beside her, taking her in his arms. He held her until she stopped shaking. In Josh's arms, she knew she was safe, and she wished she could stay like this forever. Then all too soon he pulled her from him and she was back to feeling vulnerable. But she daren't let herself depend on him too much.

'I'm sorry you had to go through that,' he said. 'But unfortunately, you are the only one who came near to seeing him. I just hope he doesn't realise that, or you may be at risk. So you must promise me you will be extra careful about going anywhere alone.'

She nodded, trying to wipe her eyes on her apron. Josh handed her a pristine white handkerchief which she gratefully accepted, scrubbing away her tears. She looked up into his eyes and found she couldn't look away. Then his eyes dropped to her mouth and she sensed that he was going to kiss her. A glow of anticipation flowed through her body, even though she knew she daren't allow it. As his lips softly caressed her own, she took a sharp intake of breath and quickly turned away.

'Forgive me, Mel,' he said quietly. 'After what you've been through, the last thing you want is another man's advances. I wasn't thinking. I promise it won't happen again. Go back inside to your aunt. I must have a few words with Mr Browning before he goes.'

As she watched him walk away Mel was crying inside. She now knew for a certainty that she loved him, but he could never be hers. He believed she'd rebuffed him because of her attack, but that hadn't anything to do with it. She would have welcomed his advances if it wasn't for her awful secret. That secret, combined with the fact she was 'trade', meant Josh could never be hers. Mel knew she'd done the right thing but it still hurt. Now she had lost him for good. He was a man of honour and she appreciated that he'd keep his word. Well, wasn't that what she wanted, what she'd always intended? But even as she acknowledged it was for the best, the pain of her loss was as sharp as any knife thrust. She buried her head in her hands and let the tears flow. She lost track of how long she'd been sitting there when she heard her aunt calling. She hurriedly scrubbed away all traces of her tears and, snatching up the basket of fruit that she'd picked earlier, went indoors to help with the rest of the wedding preparations.

'Thanks, Mel. You alright? Would you prefer to go and lie down?' Hannah asked.

'No, I'd rather keep busy if you don't mind, Aunt Hannah. Leaves me less time to think.'

'If you're sure. There's still plenty to do, though I think I've finished most of the cooking. Just this fruit to simmer and pop into the tart cases. Oh, and I've run out of eggs. Do you think you could go over to the hen house and see if there are any more?'

Outside, in the yard, Mel eyed the geese standing next to the henhouse. She'd become quite used to them now and the gander usually left her alone. But today, something had ruffled his feathers; he was strutting around, hissing at everyone and everything. Then Mel heard raised voices by the gate. Rupert Johnson and Connor O'Flynn were arguing, and things were getting very heated. Next, Mel heard the engineer shout.

'You'd better watch your step, or you'll find yourself back in prison. And it won't be so easy to get you out next time.'

With that, the engineer turned and stomped back into the house. Mel gasped in horror. Had the engineer been responsible for the trumped-up charges that had put Connor in prison before? It very much sounded like it. But what had he against Connor that would make him do such a thing? Mel went over to where Connor was still standing by the gate, staring at Rupert's disappearing back.

'Oh Connor, that sounded as though Rupert was admitting to making false charges against you. Shouldn't we tell someone?'

Connor shook his head. 'No good, Miss Mel. He'd just deny it and make out you're in it with me. But I'm not too bothered about that. What worries me is the effect all this is having on the navvies.'

'What has he done this time?'

'He's still docking their wages to supposedly pay for lost and broken tools and equipment. But it shouldn't be the navvies that pay. It's the responsibility of the canal bosses, especially as most of the damage has been done by locals who aren't happy about the canal being dug in the first place. But what Johnson doesn't seem to realize is that he's playing with fire. The navvies will only be pushed so far before there's real trouble, and I think they are very close to that point. Anyway, it's not your worry. Have you recovered from your recent ordeal?'

'Yes, but I hope they catch the man before it happens to anyone else.'

'I'm sure they will, now they've brought in one of the Bow Street Runners,' Connor reassured her. 'Now I must get back. Be careful, mind.' As he disappeared back across the fields, Mel returned to the hen house and her job of collecting eggs. But her mind kept returning to the argument she'd overheard. She couldn't understand the engineer's attitude. Surely it was his job to ensure that the work progressed smoothly and that working conditions were trouble-free? Instead, he seemed to be deliberately stirring the navvies up. Mel just couldn't fathom why he should want to do that. If there was too much trouble, wouldn't it put his own job at risk? Or was there an alternative motive? She shook her head. It was an unanswerable question and thankfully not her problem. Putting it out of her mind, Mel took the eggs indoors.

The following day, wedding fever seemed to have infected the whole household. Tempers were getting fraught as things were mislaid or dropped, until Hannah sent all the helpers out to decorate the barn. Its bareness was soon transformed with boughs of greenery twined round poles and hung from beams. Fresh rushes were cut and strewn over the newly swept floor. Then Mel scattered sprigs of lavender and rosemary amongst them so that when the dancing began, their fragrance would fill the air. The trestle tables and benches were erected. Two chairs for the bride and groom were adorned with flowers and foliage. Mel stood back to admire their handiwork.

'It looks great, don't you think, Ruth? Ruth?'

But her friend didn't seem to have heard. She was staring at the two chairs as if she hated the sight of them.

Mel touch Ruth's arm. 'If you don't like them, we can easily change them.'

Ruth shook her head. 'I can't do it,' she blurted out.

'What d'you mean? Do what?'

'The wedding, I can't go through with it!'

Mel was shocked. She'd heard people talk about pre-wedding nerves, but she never connected Ruth with nerves of any sort. She'd always seemed so calm.

'It will be alright. All your friends will be there to support you.' Mel tried to reassure her. 'It will only take an hour or so and then it will be all over.'

Again Ruth shook her head. 'It's not the wedding itself. I don't want to get married. I want to call the whole thing off.'

'But I thought you loved Ben!'

'I do, that's why I have to call it off.'

'That doesn't make sense, Ruth. Why have you suddenly decided this?'

'Oh Mel, I had this awful dream last night. It was so real; I think it was a premonition, warning me. I've been worrying about it all day.'

Mel put her arm around her friend and, leading her to a chair, said gently, 'Come and sit down and tell me all about it. What was it about? Why do you believe it was a premonition?'

'It was so frightening. I was trapped inside a cloud of thick grey fog and couldn't get free, no matter which way I turned. I could hear you all calling to me, urging me to join you, but there was no way out. Then Ben jumped into the water and began swimming towards me, but he wasn't getting any nearer and he was tiring. I knew he was going to drown and I was unable to help him. It was awful. When I awoke I was crying. Oh, Mel, I couldn't bear anything to happen to Ben, so I must call the wedding off.' She ended with a sob.

'Oh Ruth, it was only a dream. How could it be anything else? After all, it's mid-summer. We're not likely to get any fog at this time of year, and the only deep water around here is likely to be in the canal—and goodness knows when that will be finished! No, it's just nerves caused by all the excitement of the coming wedding. After all, you hadn't expected to get married for years until this offer of a cottage was suddenly sprung on you. It's no wonder you're on edge. Don't worry, as long as you both love each other it will work out fine, you'll see.'

'Do you really think so?'

'Yes I do,' Mel told her firmly. 'Now let's go into the house and I'll make you a soothing cup of camomile tea. Then you can rest. We've done everything we can out here anyway.'

In the kitchen, Hannah took one look at Ruth's white face and bustled forward, wiping her floury hands on her voluminous apron, asking what had happened.

'Ruth wants to cancel the wedding,' Mel blurted out. 'She's been having bad dreams, Aunt Hannah.'

Hannah drew the shaking girl into her arms.

'Oh you poor lass, it's only natural for a young girl to be anxious at a time like this—especially not having a mother to guide you. But I'm sure things won't seem so bad if we talk about it. You know you can say anything to me for I already think of you as my daughter. Come upstairs and lie down while Mel heats up a drink for you.'

As Mel busied herself gathering the ingredients for Ruth's drink, she thought about Ruth's extraordinary dream. But no matter how she tried to analyse it, she just couldn't see how it could possibly predict anything. It didn't make any sense. Shaking her head, she took the tea up to Ruth. When her aunt eventually came back downstairs, she reported that Ruth had calmed down and was now sleeping.

'Don't worry, I'm sure she'll be fine in the morning. Weddings tend to start all sorts of doubts in young girls' heads. It usually works out alright in the end, but I think she should stay here tonight. Can you pop over to the vicarage and tell her father? Take old Sam with you.' Her aunt had insisted ever since her attack that, if she went anywhere outside the garden, she should take the old sheepdog with her. Mel didn't mind as she had become quite attached to him now, and he did help her confidence.

Mel was glad of the chance to get out on her own for a while; away from the hustle and bustle of the wedding preparations. It was a beautiful evening and the hay meadows were ablaze with colour. It seemed sad that in a few days' time, all these flowers would be gone – cut down with the grass to make hay. Birds were winging their way lazily across a blue sky towards their night-time roosts. The few fluffy clouds were tinged with pink. Mel remembered her uncle telling her this promised fine weather the following day. She really hoped so, for Ruth's sake.

The Rev. Crosley was working in his garden when Mel arrived, his pudding face creasing into a smile of welcome.

'Ah, salvation arrives in human form, providing me with the perfect excuse for abandoning this back-breaking task with a clear conscience. Come on in, my dear, and let us avail ourselves with a refreshing liquid.'

Mel gratefully accepted the mug of homemade lemonade while explaining why Ruth had decided to stay the night at the farm. The vicar agreed this was probably the best thing.

'I shall miss her, you know. I'm considering looking for a housekeeper,' he confided. 'I may ask Simon Hunt's widow if she'd be interested?'

Mel giggled. Audrey Hunt was an attractive widow who made no secret of the fact that she was looking for another husband. She wondered if the vicar was aware of this. Soon after, Mel called to Sam and they set off back home. She wanted to make sure she reached the farm before dark.

Much to everyone's relief, the morning of the wedding dawned bright and clear with no sign of impending rain. Ruth seemed to have regained her usual serene self. By the time the men came in for their breakfast after dealing with the livestock, the girls had already washed and were concentrating on fixing their hair.

'There's plenty of hot water, so jump to it,' Hannah said, trying to chivvy them along.

But then there was a loud knocking at the door. John opened it to find Connor O'Flynn standing there.

'One of your cows is stuck in the ditch, Mr Preston, near the canal. It has been bellowing real cruel. I don't think it can get out.'

'Thanks for letting us know, O'Flynn. That must be Long

Acre, where we put the heifers that are due to calf. Come on Ben, there's no time to lose.'

Ben was already pulling on his boots. 'I'll harness Captain to the sled in case we need more pulling power.'

'Ben! The wedding!' shrieked Ruth.

'Sorry love, it will have to wait,' he said, dropping a quick kiss on her cheek before following his father out the door.

Hannah shook her head. 'The first thing you have to learn as a farmer's wife is that the livestock always comes first. After all, they are your bread and butter. Now I think we all need a pick-me-up. I will open a bottle of my cowslip wine.'

CHAPTER 13

Ruth was restless. Her endless pacing was driving Mel mad. She suggested they went for a walk outside. Ruth readily agreed.

'Don't go far. The men should be back any time now,' Hannah warned.

'It should be fun creating your own garden,' Mel suggested, leading her through her own beloved herb garden. 'I believe the one at the cottage is very overgrown at the minute. Have you thought about what you'll plant there?

'I know nothing about gardening,' Ruth admitted, continuing as Mel expressed surprise, 'Oh, I know the names of flowers from when I paint them. But I've never thought about growing any.'

'Who did the Rectory garden? Your father?'

'Some of it, but mostly he managed to persuade one of his parishioners to do it. I was never expected to do anything other than light housework. Father employed a cook and a woman to do the laundry. That's one reason why I'm so scared about this wedding—I don't know how I shall cope. Ben is sure to be disappointed. His mother is very efficient.'

Mel was shocked that her friend had so little preparation

for this wedding. It seemed that she had immersed herself in her art to the exclusion of everything else. Was Ben even aware of this? Mel hoped he'd be patient with Ruth.

'Don't worry; it's surprising how quickly one can adjust to a different way of life. Aunt Hannah will help you. I remember how scared I was when I first arrived here. I'd never even seen the countryside before. Everything was so vast and overpowering. Even Sam here frightened the life out of me,' she said, patting the old dog's head as he looked up at her with adoring eyes. 'All I wanted to do was run back to Birmingham and hide. Now I'd hate to live anywhere else.'

'Do you really believe I can do it?'

'Of course you can.' Mel assured her friend. 'Just don't be afraid to ask for help. If you want to start a herb garden, I can give you some of these plants.' She proceeded to identify various ones, explaining their uses and adding some of the mistakes she'd made during her own learning curve. Soon she was relieved to see Ruth relax and even laugh with her. They made their way round to the yard where they could see across the fields. The gander showed his annoyance at their presence but Mel now confidently waved him away. The girls both laughed at the way, after a final hiss, he stuck his beak up in the air and strutted off, his wives waddling after him, all arguing amongst themselves. Just then, Josh arrived with his gig. He'd offered to drive Ruth and John to the church and bring the bride and groom back. The rest would be happy to walk as it wasn't far across the field.

'What's this? Is the wedding off?' he asked, seeing the girls still in their everyday clothes. But when he'd heard the explanation, he offered to drive over to the church and warn the vicar that there would be a bit of delay. Then, as he left, the men were spotted returning across the fields.

'They'll be here soon, Ruth. We'd best go in now and get dressed. Do you feel better now?'

'Yes, thank you, Mel. Talking to you has helped me. I will try and follow your example and embrace my new life with optimism. Let's go.'

Hand in hand they ran back into the farmhouse.

Having reported that the heifer was now free and thankfully seemed no worse for her ordeal, the men went off to get washed and changed. The girls had just slipped on their dresses when Hannah came into their room, dressed in her best purple silk. She handed Ruth a beautiful soft silk shawl embroidered with green and blue flowers, giving her a quick hug.

'Just a little gift for you, my dear. Wishing you all the best for the future.'

Ruth's eyes glistened with unshed tears as she stammered her thanks.

'Now girls, let's see how you look. Give us a twirl, Ruth. My, she looks beautiful, don't you think, Mel?'

Mel agreed. The sky blue dress with its lace collar emphasized Ruth's blue eyes. Her long blonde hair flowed freely down her back like silvered moonlight. Mel carefully placed the coronet of wildflowers that they had made together on her head.

'I've added to your coronet some sprigs of lavender for lasting love, and some thyme for courage,' Mel told her.

Ruth laughed. 'You and your herbs,' she teased. 'Well, I hope they work, for at the moment I feel in need of both.'

Hannah patted her future daughter-in-law's hand. 'Don't you worry, dear. I'm sure everything will be fine.' Then she turned to Mel. 'And you're looking grand yourself,' she said. 'That apple green dress compliments your copper curls nicely. What are you wearing on your head?'

'As I'm acting as Ruth's hand-maiden, I trimmed my straw bonnet with the same wildflowers as are in her headdress.'

'That's fine. I'm very proud of you both.' Just then there was a rat-tat-tat on their door and John put his head around it.

'If you ladies have finished preening your feathers, Josh is at the door waiting to take Ruth and myself to the church. So the rest of you had best get a move on.'

It only took five minutes to walk across to the church and they were all in their seats by the time Josh drew up outside. The little church was packed, and many more of the villagers were waiting outside ready to escort the bride and groom back to the farm for the wedding feast. Even Lord and Lady Benchard and Fleur were there, though Mel thought Lady Benchard was looking very frail. Mel waited at the door, ready to lead her uncle and the bride down the aisle to where Ben, looking unusually smart in spotless buff breeches, dark blue frock coat, and green and blue waistcoat, was waiting nervously. He'd been casting many anxious glances at the door as if he couldn't really believe Ruth was coming. But when he saw her, the look on his face told everyone just how much he loved his bride. Ruth's father conducted a very moving service and Mel could feel tears pricking her eyes. Would she ever be a bride? Sadly, she thought it very unlikely. She loved the wrong man.

Outside the church, everyone gathered round the happy couple, offering their congratulations. Mel noticed Fleur standing slightly apart, and as she hadn't seen her lately, decided to go over and speak to her.

'Don't you talk to me, you traitor,' Fleur spat at her.

Mel was shocked. What could she possibly have done to deserve that sort of greeting?

'Fleur – what d'you mean? I'm your friend.'

'That's what I thought until Rupert told me how you were always poking your nose in where it wasn't wanted. And now you've brought that lawman from London down on us. I hate you.'

'But – I don't understand. Don't you want that killer caught?'

'Of course I do. But he's not only investigating those attacks. He keeps nosing around in places where he has no right to. He'll spoil everything and it's all your fault. Rupert was right all along. You're just a jealous busybody.'

Mel gasped as what Fleur was saying sank in.

'It's Rupert you're in love with, isn't it, Fleur? Not some boy in the next village. Why did you tell me that?'

'So that you wouldn't go blurting it out to Josh, of course.'

'But he's much older than you, Fleur. Surely the fact that you have to keep it secret must tell you it's not right?'

'It *is* right. We love each other. I know you don't like him, but you would if you got to know him better. He's so intelligent and clever. He will be famous one day. This canal is only the beginning of his career. Men have made great names for themselves as canal engineers, and he's going to as well. So you keep your nose out of our business in future.'

'Fleur, I really think you should—'

'Don't try and tell me what I should do! And stop running after my brother. He will never marry you, you know. Josh is promised to Lady Carolyn Flemming-Smythe, and she's a proper lady, not some trumped-up 'trade' hussy.' With that, she swung round on her heel and joined her parents entering their coach. Mel stood there in a daze. What had Fleur meant about the lawman's investigations spoiling everything? Had the engineer something to hide? Whatever did Fleur see in him? Still, who was she to criticize someone for falling for the wrong man? Hadn't she done just that herself? Her aunt came over to her.

'Are you alright, Mel? Were you and Fleur arguing?'

'It's nothing, Aunt Hannah. Just a silly girlish tiff,' Mel told her.

'Then come along. We need to get back to the farm and make sure Martha Carter and her helpmates have laid out the food properly.'

There was a buzz of excitement as family and friends filled the old barn. Gatherings like this were few and far between in the country, and everyone was determined to make the most of it. Josh was there—having brought the bride and groom—but his parents, because of Lady Benchard's health, had gone home. Mel was relieved to find that Fleur had gone with them. She didn't want any more unpleasant scenes spoiling Ruth's day.

The food was soon depleted. Everyone agreed that Hannah was an excellent cook, though Hannah said it was the quantity of her homemade wines consumed that had convinced them. This was received with much good-natured laughter. After the usual speeches, the tables were pushed back and two of the local musicians brought out their fiddles. They soon had people's feet tapping, and there were shouts for Ben and Ruth to start the dancing. Ben cavorted rather clumsily around the floor with Ruth, who was blushing charmingly as she tried to keep up with him.

'I don't think dancing is one of Ben's better points,' Josh laughed. 'Shall we take pity on them and join in?' Mel readily agreed, pleased that Josh was so considerate. Soon many others were up on their feet as well, and the festivities continued in full swing. Eventually, as many farmers had animals to deal with, things began to wind down. The bride and groom were escorted to their cottage with much ribald joking. Everyone agreed it had been a delightful wedding.

The following week seemed very flat after the excitement. It was soon obvious to everyone that Ruth and Ben were very happy and relaxed about their marriage. Ruth had clearly put all her fears about her dream right out of her mind, but Mel still had an uneasy feeling about it. However, life on a farm never stood still. As the fine weather was still holding, preparations were being made to start haymaking. The screech of scythe blades being sharpened on the whet-stone jarred Mel's ears. She tried to do her bit by sorting out the wooden rakes that would be used to toss the hay. Mel was excited, having never seen haymaking before, and was keen to be involved as much as possible. Her aunt laughed, telling her that by the time she'd finished tossing a field of drying grass—which was apparently women's work—she'd think differently. As many men with scythes as possible were needed for cutting the hay, and Mel was surprised when two gypsies turned up to help. Evidently, this small band of gypsies turned up each year, and Lord Benchard always allowed them to set up camp on his land. Some gypsies had a bad reputation, but this group came every year and was never any trouble. Her uncle was very pleased to see them this year, as all the local casual labourers were busy working on the canal and this left many of the farmers struggling with the seasonal work. The following morning, the men began cutting the grass. It would be a long job so, at lunchtime, Hannah asked Ruth and Mel to take some pasties and earthenware jugs of ale out to them to save time. Ruth had been used to seeing the haymaking all her life, but to Mel, it was very new. She was fascinated as she watched the men, strung out in a staggered line across the field, swinging their big scythes in unison.

Ruth laughed at her. 'You wait 'til tomorrow when you have to help toss the grass . . .'

'What, do they just pick it up and throw it around? Whatever for?' Mel asked.

'To let the air get through it. It helps it dry quicker. But we don't throw it anywhere, silly. We use wooden rakes to turn it over and then pile it into small heaps that we call hay-cocks so that it can finish drying. If it's going to last through the winter, it has to be completely dry.'

'So you've done this before.'

'No, I haven't actually, though I've seen them doing it. But Ben was explaining it all to me last night. Part of my education into being a farmer's wife.' She finished with a giggle.

Mel was pleased to see her friend so happy and relaxed. She was obviously prepared to wholeheartedly enter into her new role. It certainly suited her; this new, bright, cheerful Ruth was very different from the quiet, reserved girl that Mel had first known. When the men had finished their lunch the two girls made their way, arm in arm, back to the farm for their own.

The following day it was the women's turn. It was a first for Mel, and she relished the thrill of it. The scents of the newly cut grass, the various perfumes from the flowers that had flourished amongst it, the warmth of the sun on her back, and the sound of the skylarks serenading them from way above in the clear blue sky. But wielding those wooden rakes all day was tiring, and she was glad when the time came to return to the farmhouse for the evening meal. Being unused to this type of work, both Ruth and Mel were suffering from aching shoulders and back, so Mel raided her store of herbal salves to rub into the painful areas. These certainly helped and the following morning, after a good night's sleep, the girls were willing to resume their haymaking duties. At last, all the fields were cut and the hay was drying nicely. Then Ben harnessed Captain and Boxer to the big wagons and collected up all the small haycocks.

'What do they do with it now?' Mel asked.

'They will be taken to the rickyard at the back of the barns, where we stack it into neat circular ricks with tapered tops,' Hannah explained. 'Then we wait for the thatcher to come and thatch a roof on them all. This will keep the hay dry until it's needed to feed the animals in the winter.'

'It seems an awful lot of work. Why can't the animals carry on just eating the grass?'

Hannah laughed. 'Your city roots are showing,' she teased. 'Everything dies back in the winter and the fields get very muddy. Without the hay to keep the animals going, they wouldn't survive until spring.'

'Seems I've still got a lot to learn,' she muttered.

Her aunt patted her back. 'Don't be too hard on yourself, love. You've only been with us a few months and you've already picked up a lot. Why, you wouldn't say boo to a goose—literally!—when you arrived. Now you're no longer afraid of the animals, and look how much you've learnt about the herbs and their uses.'

'That's because I find the subject so fascinating. They can be used for so many different things. There's so much more I want to learn about them.'

'That's good. It's a very worthwhile subject to study; especially in the country, where we haven't got access to trained apothecaries. Now, let's help the men wind up this haymaking. We've been lucky that the weather has stayed fine, but I reckon it won't last much longer.'

In another couple of days, it was all wrapped up. This was to everyone's relief because, as the air got hotter and stickier, it was soon obvious a change was on its way. John and Hannah thanked everyone for their hard work and Hannah then suggested the two girls took the whole day off as a reward.

'Ruth and Ben can join us for our evening meal, so Ruth can enjoy a free day. And that includes you, Mel.'

'I shall take the opportunity to do some painting,' Ruth told Mel when she asked. 'I haven't picked up a paintbrush since the wedding. It will be good to get back to it. What about you, Mel? Will you be concocting more magic with your herbs?'

Mel laughed. 'I don't know about the magic bit but I do need to replenish my stock of salves. We used up quite a few during the haymaking.'

And so the two friends cheerfully went their separate ways. Mel spent some happy moments perusing through her herb garden, picking the ones she knew she would use. By then the weather had turned very hot and muggy, and she was glad to step into the relative cool of her still room. She lost all sense of time as she shredded, pounded, mixed and potted the herbs into her various salves. So she was surprised when Ben poked his head round the door.

'Mel, Ruth hasn't come back yet. Would you mind going and giving her a warning that there's a storm about to break? I expect she's so wrapped up in her painting that she hasn't even noticed. I believe she was going up to the East Wood. I'd go myself but I need to finish the milking.'

'Of course, I hadn't noticed the time either. I could do with stretching my legs.'

She hurried out through the yard, collecting Sam on the way. She still felt happier with the faithful old dog at her side. As she opened the gate to the field there was a thunderclap but no rain. Mel shuddered. She remembered that last thunderstorm she was caught out in and wished she could run back indoors.

But she'd promised Ben, so she kept going. The rain started to plop in fat drops on her shoulders. Surely Ruth would be on her way back by now? Mel quickened her pace.

But when she got near the wood, Ruth was nowhere to be seen. Then she noticed her paints and paper scattered about the grass. Where was she? Had she gone into the wood for something? But if so, why had she left her paintings lying about on the grass? Mel's heart started racing.

CHAPTER 14

'Ruth, where are you?' Mel shouted, only to be answered by a terrific crash of thunder. Mel screamed and huddled down on the ground frozen, her head in her arms and there was nowhere to hide. Then the rain began in earnest, drenching her in seconds. Still she stayed as she was, trembling in fright. Sam nudged her, poking his nose under her arm. The thunder rumbled on; bright flashes of lightning lit up the dark trees of the wood behind her, reminding her that she needed to find Ruth. Had she gone in there for shelter?

'Oh Sam, I can't go in there. Find Ruth, Sam. Go and find her.' She pushed him away but the bewildered dog just looked back at her. 'Go fetch Ruth,' she repeated, knowing that was the command for him to round up the sheep. Would he understand? He looked at the wood and then back at her. She waved her hand at him, and at last, he took off, disappearing into the trees. Another crash of thunder had her quivering with fear, unable to move, hating herself for being such a coward when she should be searching for her friend. After what seemed hours, but was probably only minutes, she heard something crashing through the trees and Sam began barking furiously.

He only ever barked like that at strangers which meant there must be someone else in there besides Ruth. But who? Her mind flashed back to her ordeal in the barn and she felt sick at the thought. Sam was back at her side, whimpering and pushing into her leg. At least he was no longer barking so Mel hoped that meant the stranger had fled. Sam ran back and forth between the wood and herself. He must have found Ruth and was asking Mel to follow him. As she hadn't appeared her friend obviously needed help and Mel must go with Sam into the wood. Luckily the thunder was now rumbling off into the distance, so taking a deep breath, she stood up and shakily followed the dog, determined to find her friend.

The storm had robbed the woods of any brightness and Mel had to pause to let her eyes adjust to the gloom. Sam was still running back and forth and his barking led her further amongst the trees. Then Mel saw Ruth. She was lying on the ground, her clothes in disarray. It was obvious she had been attacked and as Mel dropped to her knees beside her friend's still body, she felt sick. Was she dead? Taking up her hand, she was shocked at how icy and limp it felt. In despair, she gently brushed a leaf from her face. Ruth flinched and her eyes flickered. She was alive. Tears of relief streamed down Mel's face. She straightened her clothes and tried to rouse her. The only response she got was more flickering of the eyes. Then Ruth opened them fully, but the vacant look they held frightened Mel. She had to get Ruth help, get her back to the farm as soon as possible. She tried to lift her into a sitting position but Ruth stayed completely limp and Mel couldn't lift her.

'Oh, come on, Ruth, please help me,' she pleaded, shaking her. But there was still no response. 'Ruth, please, we need to get you back to the farm and I can't manage it without your help.' The more Mel tried, the more frustrated she became. At last, she gave up. It was no good, she needed to get help. But how? If she went to the farm herself, the villain who had attacked Ruth might still be out there. He might come back and finish her off. If that happened, Mel knew she would never forgive herself. No, she couldn't risk that. She had to think of another way, but what? Sam was nudging Ruth's arm with his nose and whining. Even he knew something was wrong. Looking at the dog, she realised Sam was her only hope. She had to send him for help. It was a gamble but it was all she could think of. But she needed some way of conveying the urgency of the situation. Then, seeing Ruth's torn shawl lying amongst the undergrowth, she had an idea. Dashing out to where her art equipment was scattered about, she snatched up a couple of the paintbrushes and, back in the wood, she tied a strip of the shawl around the brushes and then tied it all round Sam's neck.

'Well, it's up to you now, boy. Go home,' she commanded him. He looked at Ruth and back to her. 'Oh please Sam, we're relying on you. Go home. Go fetch Ben, go on.' She pushed him away, waving her arms. However, Sam seemed reluctant to leave them. In desperation, Mel repeatedly issued the same command. At last, with one more look at Ruth, he turned and ran off. Thankfully, she sank back down beside Ruth, praying that the dog would go straight to the farm and that someone there would recognise the significance of the paintbrushes he was carrying. As she settled back down beside Ruth, she rubbed her cold hands, continually talking quietly to her, even though she had no idea if she could hear her.

The wait seemed endless. Mel jumped nervously at every sound in the wood, every bird that fluttered in the trees, every branch that rustled in the wind, thinking it could be the villain coming back. Was he still in the vicinity, perhaps even watching them? Still, Ruth didn't move. Had Sam gone straight to the farm? Had anyone seen him? What would she do if no help came? Mel felt quite sick with worry, but she knew she must stay strong for her friend's sake. At last, she heard her uncle calling her. Sobbing with relief, she stumbled to the edge of the wood, where she found both her uncle and Ben.

'Where's Ruth? What's happened,' Ben demanded, running up to her. Wordlessly she turned and led them back to where Ruth lay. With a cry, Ben dropped down beside her and gathered her into his arms.

John touched Mel's arm. 'Is she . . . I mean . . . She's not . . .?' he asked, stumbling over the words.

Mel shook her head. 'No, she alive – just. Oh, uncle, I couldn't rouse her. I didn't know how to get her home,' she sobbed.

'You did well. When we saw her shawl and paintbrushes tied to Sam, we knew something was wrong. That was very clever of you. Now, let's get you both home.'

Between them, the two men managed to get Ruth up, and John lifted her into his arms. Ben took Mel's arm and they all made their way back through the rain to the farm. Luckily for Mel, the thunder had passed over; it was now merely a muted rumble in the distance. As the farmhouse came into sight, John told Ben to run on ahead and warn his mother to get a bed ready for Ruth.

'I think it will be better if we care for Ruth in the farmhouse until she's better, rather than at your cottage. It will be easier to keep an eye on her when you're out at work all day,' he told his son.

With only a nod, Ben rushed off.

When they entered the farm kitchen, Hannah was anxiously waiting for them.

'The poor thing. I've made up the truckle bed for her in the front room and I've got the water heating up on the hearth, so take her straight through,' Hannah told them.

As John laid her carefully on the bed, Ruth groaned, causing everyone to sigh with relief. At least she was still alive.

'Now, you men, make yourself scarce while Mel and I get these wet clothes off her and make her comfortable.'

Ben moved to the bed and took Ruth's limp hand in his strong, tanned one.

'Oh Mum, I can't bear to see her like this. Will she be alright, d'you think?'

'We will do our best for her, son. You must give her time to heal. Now go and bring in a bowl of hot water and then finish your chores outside, there's a good lad.'

'If I ever find who did this, I swear I'll kill him,' he declared when he returned with the water.

'Now, now, there's no need to do anything rash.' His mother told him. 'I'm sure the authorities will catch him soon.'

'Unfortunately, not soon enough,' he muttered on his way out.

'Are you up to this, Mel?' Hannah asked, noticing her niece's white, tear-streaked face for the first time.

Mel nodded. 'Yes, it's just that it's reminded me too vividly of my own experience. Though I realize I was a lot luckier than poor Ruth. I do hope she recovers from it.'

'We all do, love. Now go and fetch some of your lavender oil to put in this water. It will take away any smell of the villain, as well as its healing properties. Oh, and you'd better bring some salves for these bruises,' Hannah added, as she pulled back Ruth's bodice, exposing the angry purple marks covering her neck and chest. By the time Mel returned, she'd removed her shoes and stockings. Together they eased off the rest of her clothes and sponged her body with the hot, sweet-scented water. It was only while they were smoothing the healing salves over her battered body, did Ruth give any indication that she was even aware that they were helping her. Then, the painful bruises brought a strangled moan from her bloodless lips. Hannah managed to get her to sip some camomile tea to help her sleep. Then, finally, now dressed in Hannah's best flannel nightshirt, and covered with several blankets, they allowed Ben to come in.

'How is she?' he asked anxiously, gazing down at Ruth's still, white face. 'She . . . She's not dead, is she?'

'No, my dear, just suffering from a severe shock,' his mother explained. 'You must be patient and give her time, but I'm sure she'll get over it. For now, we must let her sleep. I'll sit with her. You go and finish your chores. You can sit with her later if you wish.'

'Oh Mum, why did this happen? We were so happy.'

'Why does any tragedy happen? We don't know, son. We just have to pray for guidance and then cope with whatever life hands us the best we can. But I'm sure in time you'll find that happiness again. Now out you go, the pair of you, and let Ruth sleep.

The next few days were anxious times but gradually Ruth rallied and, after a week, she declared herself well enough to go back to her cottage and resume a normal life again.

'But she's not back to normal, is she?' Mel perceived later that week. 'Where is that happy bubbly girl she became after the wedding?'

Her Aunt shook her head sadly. 'No, she seems to have reverted back to the quiet, reserved girl she was. I think it will be a long time before she really gets over it – if ever. Trouble is, it's affecting Ben too. He's become very moody, just when he needs to be showing patience and understanding. Oh, how I wish that dratted canal had never come to our area.'

Later that week, Mel was churning the butter in the dairy when Rupert Johnson put his head round the door.

'Ah, that's where you are. I've been looking for you,' he said.

Mel looked up in surprise. Ever since their last disagreement, the engineer had made a point of avoiding her, and when this hadn't been possible he'd just ignored her.

'I thought you'd like to know they've caught the villain who attacked your friend,' He continued.

'Oh, that's good news.'

'Yes, it was one of those filthy gypsies who are camped out in the manor's woods. Now you can tell your nosy friend to go back to London and leave us to get on with the job of building this canal.'

'He's not . . .' But he had gone before Mel could point out that the Bow Street Runner was Josh's friend, not hers. Mel sighed. As she patted the butter into individual blocks as her aunt had taught her, she mulled over the news. She should have been relieved, but she'd been convinced it was one of the canal navvies. However, the authorities must know their job. She decided to take a pat of butter over to Ruth and tell her the news. The back door was open and she found Ruth on her hands and knees, scrubbing away at the stone-flagged floor as though it hadn't been scrubbed for years. Yet it looked spotless, as was the rest of the little cottage.

'Hello Ruth, I've brought some butter over for you. Oh, your poor hands,' Mel exclaimed as Ruth stood and took the butter from her. 'I'll make up a special salve for you to rub into them. But you should really keep them out of water for a bit.'

'Oh, I can't do that. With all the dirt Ben brings in from the farm, I need to make sure the house is clean.'

'It looks spotless now, Ruth, so I'm sure if you let up for a few days it wouldn't matter.'

'What d'you know about it? You know nothing. Don't try and tell me what I should or shouldn't do. Now please go.' Ruth snapped at her.

Mel stared at her friend in dismay. This wasn't the Ruth she had come to like and respect. With a sob, she turned and left.

That evening, Mel told her aunt and uncle of her visit to Ruth.

'Oh Aunt Hannah, you should see her hands—they're so red and raw. I don't think she could even hold a paintbrush now, much less paint a picture. Why has she suddenly become so obsessive about cleaning?'

'It seems to me that that man made her feel dirty and this is her reaction – her way of coping with it,' her aunt explained. 'Unfortunately, I've no idea how to stop it. I've tried to talk to her about it but she just changes the subject. It's such a shame, for they were so happy.'

'Trouble is, it's affecting Ben as well.' John said. 'I'm told he spends every evening drinking in the tavern.'

'Surely not too much?' His wife protested.

John shook his head sadly. 'Too much, wife! He's practically drowning himself in it.'

Mel gasped. 'Drowning! Oh no—it's the dream!'

Her aunt and uncle looked at her in surprise. 'What dream? What are you talking about, Mel?'

'Didn't she tell you, Aunt Hannah? Just before the wedding, Ruth had this awful dream that really scared her. She said she was trapped in a thick grey fog and couldn't get out of it, although she could hear us all calling her. Then Ben jumped into a lake to save her, but he couldn't reach her and was drowning. She said it was so vivid it was almost like a premonition. She nearly called off the wedding but I persuaded her not to. Oh, Aunt Hannah, did I do wrong?'

'Don't blame yourself, dear. I'm sure we would all have done the same. I have to admit I can see the parallels in this situation, but that doesn't tell us what we should do now.' She finished with a despairing sigh.

'I don't think there is anything we can do. Time often has a habit of sorting things out,' John said. 'We just need to make sure we're always there if they need us. Also, we need to pray.'

Early the next morning Mel was in her herb garden, determined to prepare a very special salve for Ruth's poor hands. As she wandered through the garden selecting a leaf here and a flower there, she became aware of someone watching her from over the hedge. It was one of the gypsy women who had helped with the haymaking. She had a small baby wrapped in a shawl across her chest.

'Hello, did you want something?' Mel asked.

'Please miss, can you help us? I don't know who else to ask.'

Mel could see then that the woman had been crying. 'What is it? Is it the baby? I might have some herbal remedy that could help,' she offered.

'No, Miss, not the baby. It's my man. They have arrested him. They say he attacked the young lady. But he would never do a thing like that, not Seth. He's the gentlest of men. I know gypsies have a bad name, but our group has always kept out of trouble. Well, save for poaching the odd rabbit now and again. But the Lord always turns a blind eye at that, 'cause he knows us. That's why he allows us to camp on his land every year. We respect that. So you see, none of us would ever do anything like what that London man is accusing us of.'

'I have to admit I was surprised when I heard they'd arrested one of yours. When they were helping us with the hay, I never felt threatened. What made them decide it was your man?'

'They said there was a witness and he swore it was Seth. They wouldn't listen when I tried to tell them he'd been with me the whole time. I know he's innocent, Miss. You must help us.'

'I'm not sure I can do much, but I'll make enquiries. I can't promise anything, mind.' Mel told her.

'Oh thank you, Miss. I knew you had a good heart.'

Then she was gone, as silently as she had come. Mel finished collecting the required herbs and took them through to the still room. While she was preparing the salve, she mulled over what the gypsy woman had told her. It did sound rather too convenient, and she was sure that the gypsies weren't in the area when she herself was attacked. Mel decided she would have a word with Josh about it tomorrow if he was at church, because, if they hadn't arrested the right man, that meant the real villain was still out there.

CHAPTER 15

The following Sunday, Mel was dismayed to find that nobody from the manor was in church. She needed to talk to Josh urgently, before it was too late, for she was convinced they'd arrested the wrong man. She twisted around so often to see if he was coming, her aunt reprimanded her. However, she found it difficult to keep still when she believed an innocent man could be hanged. They were singing the first hymn when Mel sighed with relief as the church door opened and Josh ushered his parents into their pew. She was surprised to see Fleur wasn't with them. After the service, she asked Josh if Fleur was ill. Josh shook his head.

'No, she's fine. She just decided she didn't want to come. She seems to spend a lot of time lately either in her room or riding her pony around the countryside. I did wonder if she was seeing a boy, but I can't think who it would be. I expect she's just at that awkward age.'

Mel wondered if she should mention Fleur's confession regarding Rupert Johnson, but decided not to betray her confidence. A decision she would later regret.

'But how are you?' Josh continued. 'Are you up for trying another driving lesson?'

'That would be lovely,' Mel said with surprise. 'With so much happening lately, I'd forgotten about that.'

'Would next Wednesday afternoon be alright? I think you need at least two more lessons before I'd let you out on your own. At least everyone should be safer now they've arrested the attacker.'

'Oh yes, but are you sure they've got the right man? Those gypsies helped us with the haymaking and not once did I feel threatened.'

'It's all cut and dried, I'm afraid. A witness has come forward who actually saw the man attacking Ruth.'

'That's strange. When we arrived, I didn't see anyone else. Neither did Sam, or he would have barked. And if someone else was there, why didn't he come forward to help us? I couldn't lift her, so I had to send Sam back to the farm for help while I stayed to watch over her. I saw or heard no one until Ben and Uncle John turned up. So who was this witness?'

'I don't know, but it sounds as though this needs looking into again. I know it's awful having to go through it again, but would you be prepared to tell the authorities what you've just told me?'

'Of course. Especially as I'm sure it wasn't a gypsy who attacked me—they weren't even in the area then.'

'Not that we know of, but I will find out and let you know Wednesday. In the meantime, take care,' he warned her. Then they went their separate ways.

* * *

'Are you alright, Mel?' her aunt asked the next morning. 'You seem very quiet.'

'I'm worried, Aunt Hannah. Have you heard they've arrested one of the gypsies?'

'Yes, I must admit I was surprised. I know gypsies often have a bad name, but that particular band has been coming here for years and we've never had any trouble from them before.'

'The man's wife waylaid me in the herb garden the other day. She's adamant that he would never hurt anyone. She asked me to help. Oh, Aunt Hannah, she had a young baby with her.'

'But what did she expect you to do?'

'I don't know. I did mention it to Josh after church yesterday. He said he'd look into it.'

They were interrupted by the sound of shouting out in the yard. Hannah sighed.

'Oh dear, Ben and John are at it again.'

'Why? I've never heard Uncle John lose his temper before. I always thought he was a very placid man.'

Hannah sadly shook her head. 'It's that wretched canal they're building. It's caused more upsets in the local families than in the whole time I've lived here.'

Her uncle stormed into the kitchen, slamming the door behind him. 'If that lad doesn't stop spending all his time in the tavern, I shall have to banish him from the farm altogether. He's a danger to himself and the animals in the state he's in.'

'Oh John, you can't!' his wife implored. 'He's just going through a difficult time with Ruth. He'll get over it.'

'I know that, but he needs to act like a man and support Ruth, not escape into the bottle. I am very disappointed in him.'

'I'll go over and see Ruth and see if I can talk to her. Though I don't know if she'll listen,' Mel added as she remembered her last visit to the cottage. Out in the yard, she found Ben huddled down by the water pump, looking very sorry for himself. He tried to stand but then gave up and sank back down again.

'Oh Ben, look at you. You must pull yourself together. Uncle John is talking about banning you from the farm, and I know you don't want that.'

'Don't care. Don't care about anything,' he mumbled.

'Come on, Ben. This isn't like you. I used to think you were strong enough to cope with anything. Think of Ruth.'

'My Ruth has gone. This Ruth hates me. Oh, Mel, we were so happy. Now she won't let me as much as put my arm round her. I don't think she even likes me in the house. She says I bring dirt in from the farm. She's forever scrubbing and polishing everything. The only place I feel welcome is the tavern. Do you blame me for spending all my time there?'

Mel was horrified to see tears on his cheeks. But could anyone blame him when Ruth was pushing him away? If only she could get through to Ruth. Determined to try, she left Ben still hugging the pump. Mel decided to take Ruth another herb cutting for her garden but Ruth refused it.

'I don't do gardening. It brings too much dirt indoors,' she explained. 'Anyway, I haven't got time to waste on that.'

'Oh, I thought you were so keen to grow your own herbs.' Mel looked at the weedy plot that Ruth had originally begun to cultivate. 'I can plant this for you if you like, and tidy it up the patch up at the same time.'

'Leave it alone. I don't need your help.'

'Ruth, you do need help. You need to talk about all this. You're driving poor Ben to drink.'

'Ben doesn't understand. He only thinks of himself. If he wants to spend all his time up the tavern, then that's no concern of mine. Now, just go away and leave us alone.'

Mel shook her head sadly as Ruth retreated back inside, slamming the door behind her. Ruth had changed out of all recognition since the attack, and Mel could see no end to it. Would she ever be her old loving, serene self again, or had that person gone forever? Was there any hope for their marriage? Mel wished she could get her hands on the man who'd done this. Though she was still not convinced that the gypsy who had been arrested was that person.

When Josh picked Mel up on Wednesday for her driving lesson, the first thing she asked was if any progress had been made regarding the witness.

Josh shook his head. 'I'm afraid not. All anyone seems to know is that if it wasn't the gypsy, it must have been one of the navvies. But which one is anyone's guess. Not an easy task with the hundreds of navvies working at the canal site. So I'm afraid they'll just plump for the only person they have.'

'What if I'm prepared to stand up and say what I know?'

'Sorry Mel, you'd be clutching at straws. As things stand, unless we have solid proof that the witness is unreliable, the magistrate is going to treat it as a cut-and-dried case.'

'But I'm sure they've got the wrong man.'

'That's as may be, but unless something new comes up I don't think there is much we can do about it. Now, forget about that and take the reins. Let's see if you've remembered everything from your last lesson.' But just as Josh was about to hand over control to Mel, she shouted.

'Stop!'

Startled, Josh tugged on the reins, causing the horse to swerve. By the time he had got the horse under control and stationary, Mel had already jumped down and was racing across the field to where two men appeared to be attacking a third. Worried about her safety, Josh shouted as loud as he could. The attackers heard him and ran off, leaving the third man on the ground. When Mel reached him she was dismayed to discover that it was Connor O'Flynn. He looked in a pretty bad way, but at least he was conscious. Josh joined them as soon as he'd tethered the horse.

'What's happened here, O'Flynn? I thought you were on the same side as the navvies. So what prompted this?'

Connor struggled to sit up. 'Jus' coming . . . to . . . see, to . . . see . . . you, sir,' he managed to get out before slumping back again.

'Don't try and talk now. Let's get you patched up first. The farm's nearest. Is it OK to take him back there, Mel?' She agreed and together they got him up into the gig. 'Now, you're going to drive us home while I make sure no one falls off. Are you up to it?'

'Yes, I think so,' she told him. 'I'll take it slowly.'

As they drove into the yard, John came running out. What now? Oh my goodness, bring him in.'

With both men supporting him, Connor managed to make it into the farm kitchen while Mel ran to the still room to fetch her salves and tinctures. She was soon back bearing various jars and bottles.

'It's a good job I made a new batch recently, though I didn't expect to use them so soon,' she told Connor whilst gently smoothing the healing salves into the various cuts and bruises on his face.

Hannah came in and sighed. 'Oh goodness, what now?' she asked, then continued without waiting for an explanation. 'Mel, go and put some water onto boil while we apply these salves to his back and chest.' By the time she returned with a hot herbal drink for him, Connor was looking a lot brighter.

'Do you feel up to talking now? Can you tell us what it was all about?' Josh asked.

Connor nodded.

'I was coming to see you, Sir, about something I'd overheard. I suspect someone else realised this and had intended to stop me. They would have managed it too if you hadn't come along at that moment. I'm very grateful to you for that. They took me by surprise and had floored me before I even realized they were there.'

'It must have been something important for them to go to all this trouble.'

'I think it could be. I overheard Wily Wilks boasting about making easy money. Of course, the others wanted to know how. Then he said all he had to do was to swear that he'd seen one of the gypsies attacking a girl. He then admitted he hadn't, but as they weren't to know that, he wasn't going to miss out on that sort of money. Some of the others objected but, as you know, there is no love lost between the navvies and the gypsies. However, I thought you should know because it could lead to an innocent man being blamed.'

'I knew it!' Mel exclaimed. 'I knew it wasn't one of the gypsies.'

'Have you any idea who it was that put this Wilkes up to this? Who was prepared to pay out money to make this accusation stick?'

Connor shook his head. 'Sorry I couldn't discover that. I tried to push Wily into telling us, but he wouldn't be drawn. I think that was what decided the real culprit to stop me from reporting this.'

'Well, it certainly points to it being one of the navvies, but with hundreds of them to choose from, how are we ever going to discover which one?' Josh frowned. 'I'll have another word with our bow-street runner. At least now we will have to let the gypsy go. We can't prosecute a man on false evidence.'

'Good, now I must be getting back to work.' Connor stood up, thanking them all for coming to his rescue and easing his pain.

'But are you fit enough? Is it safe for you to go back? What if they have another go at you?' Mel asked.

Connor shook his head. 'The men will have already reported that I'd seen you, so there won't be much point in attacking me now. I'm feeling much better since you've patched me up, thanks, but I must get back. After all, who will look out for the welfare of the navvies if I don't? They're not all bad, you know. Most of us are good, hard-working folk trying to make a living the best way we can.' With a jaunty wave, he was on his way.

'Oh Josh, does this mean the attacker is still at large?' Hannah asked anxiously.

'It would seem so. I must follow up on this new information quickly before things get too complicated. So I'll be away.' Mel went outside with him. 'Sorry, we had to cut your driving lesson short, Mel. We'll arrange another time soon. In the meantime, promise me you'll take extra care.' With one finger, he lifted her chin and looked deep into her eyes. The air between them positively fizzed, and for one breathless moment, Mel thought he was about to kiss her. But the moment passed and he moved away, adding, 'I should hate for you to suffer the same fate as Ruth.'

'I'll be careful. Oh, Josh, do you think Ruth will ever recover from this?' she said quickly to cover her disappointment.

'I'm sure she will eventually. Time is a great healer. We must all have patience. I will do my best to delve deeper into this investigation. It seems to me that there is something else going on, besides these attacks, which is clouding the clues. But what it is, unfortunately, I've no idea.' Then he unhitched the gig and was away.

Mel felt too unsettled to go back inside, so she made her way round to her herb garden. Sitting on the bench there, she waited for her treacherous heart to settle down. She saw so little of Josh these days and had been looking forward to spending a couple of hours with him during her driving lesson. But now she'd even been denied this. However, she knew they'd had to go to Connor's assistance. Then, when Josh had tilted her chin to look deep into her eyes, she had been sure he was going to kiss her. Instead, he'd turned aside, and it had taken all of Mel's willpower not to throw her arms about his neck and beg for his kisses. Of course, she would never do that. It would be humiliating if he rejected her overtures. Anyway, it wouldn't be fair to lead him on when she knew she could never be his. However, even knowing this, her body still trembled with longing. Had he felt the magnetism as well? Or had it been all one-sided? She really should stop tormenting herself, thinking about Josh, and perhaps look elsewhere. But her heart wouldn't let her. She heard her aunt calling her and quickly went indoors.

'Come along, lass, it's no good mooning around. That won't help anyone. I thought this would be a good time to turn out the linen cupboard. If I don't do it soon, winter will be on us before we know it.' But before they could make a start, the gander's loud squawking warned them that they had a visitor.

'Now who could that be,' Hannah mused as she went to open the door. 'Why, Rev. Crossley, this is a surprise. Come in. What brings you in this direction?'

'I've just been to visit my daughter.' His usual smiling pudding face seemed to have sagged in on itself, his eyes bleak. 'Oh, Mrs Preston, that person isn't my daughter. Where is my gentle, loving little girl? How could she have changed so? I don't know what to do. I tried talking but she won't listen. She even refuses to come to church. She says God has abandoned her. But I rather think that Ruth has abandoned God. And why this obsession with cleaning? I'm at my wit's end.'

'Come and sit down. Mel, warm the Reverent some herbal tea. I'm sure Ruth will recover in time. But you must remember she's had a terrible experience. It's bound to have after-effects. She feels she has been made dirty and this is her way of coping with it. It isn't easy on Ben either. Unfortunately, he's taken refuge in strong drink, and we both know that isn't the answer.'

The vicar shook his head sadly. 'When they first told us they were going to build a canal through our village I welcomed it, thinking it would help us all prosper. Instead, it has only brought us misery and heartache.'

'But once it's finished, I'm sure it will be fine and you'll all benefit,' Mel insisted, unwilling to abandon her faith in the advantages of canals.

'Trouble is, it's a long way off being finished, and in the meantime, how many other tragedies will be left in its wake? I can only appeal to everyone to offer up prayers for those affected. Never has there been a greater need for prayer. Even my faith is being sorely tested,' the vicar finished sadly

'Don't worry, we will keep an eye on Ruth. We have grown very fond of her. I am sure everything will turn out right if we give it time,' Hannah assured him.

'Thank you for listening to me. You have given me hope that our prayers will be answered eventually. Now I mustn't take up any more of your time.' The vicar rose and shook hands with them both. 'I did hear rumours of some big contraption being brought to the canal that can do the job much quicker than the men, so maybe the end will be nearer than we thought. Let's hope so, anyway.'

CHAPTER 16

The next morning the whole village was abuzz with the news of this strange machine that was to be brought to the canal site to speed up progress. At breakfast, Hannah asked her husband if he'd heard any details.

'No, but anything that gets that blasted canal finished quickly is good. The sooner we get this village back to normal, the better,' he grumbled, shovelling bacon and eggs into his mouth. 'Mel, I shall need you this morning to help move the sheep into the lower pasture.'

'Me?' She stared at him. 'But Ben always does that.' She still wasn't completely comfortable dealing with the animals, even though she tried.

'That wretched boy isn't fit to do anything after a night down the tavern. I don't know what to do with him.'

'Oh John, the poor lad is under a lot of strain.' His mother defended him.

'I know that, but he should be home supporting Ruth instead of just drowning his sorrows. I've no patience with him.'

'Maybe if I have a word with him. Perhaps he'll listen to his mother.'

'You can try, but I doubt it will make much difference.' He snatched his cap and headed for the door. 'Come out when you're ready, Mel.'

'You'd best go, lass,' her aunt told her, noticing her reluctance. 'He'll only take it out on poor Ben otherwise.'

With the help of their sheepdog, Sam, things went much smoother than Mel expected. The sheep were all safely in their new field in no time. She was feeling quite pleased with herself as she headed back to the farmhouse, but then the jewel-bright colours of a gypsy shawl caught her eye. Turning around, she saw the gypsy woman with her baby beckoning her from the lane.

'We're moving on,' she told Mel. 'But before we leave, I wanted to thank you for helping in the release of my husband. I knew he wouldn't harm anyone.'

'I didn't really do anything,' Mel protested, 'but I'm glad it turned out alright. I understood from my uncle that you usually stayed around until after the apple picking was finished.'

'Normally we would do that, but now the suspicion has reverted to the navvies we're afraid there may be reprisals. There's never been any love lost between navvies and gypsies, so to be on the safe side we'll be moving on now.'

'I'm sorry, maybe we'll see you next year.'

'We'll be back once the canal's finished. May luck go with you and may you find your heart's desire.' Then she was gone.

Mel sighed as she thought about the gypsy's parting words. She very much doubted she'd ever achieve her heart's desire. There were too many odds stacked against that possibility.

Several days later, news filtered in that the new canal-digging machine had been installed and was up and running.

'I should like to see it. Could I walk over sometime today, Aunt Hannah?' Mel asked at breakfast time.

Her uncle paused, his forkful of bacon balanced halfway to his mouth, as he contemplated what his niece had said.

'I'm not sure that going near the canal workings on your own is such a good idea at the moment, my dear,' he reminded her.

'Oh, but I do want to see it. They say it's the only one like it ever built.' Mel begged.

'Maybe if I went with her it would be alright, John. What d'you think?' Hannah asked. 'I must admit I'm also very curious about it.'

John nodded. 'As long as you both stick together I guess it will be alright. I'd come myself if I could spare the time. It's not every day new inventions are seen around this part of the world. But with Ben still practically useless, it's impossible.'

So later that day, Mel and her aunt donned their bonnets and shawls and set off across the fields to the canal. There were quite a few villagers gathered on the edge of the canal workings. Their excited chattering and the shouts of the workers greeted the girls as they neared the site. However, all this faded into the background as the slap of wood against wood, and the unfamiliar groans and squeaks of wooden gears grinding together reached them. Intrigued, they pressed forward.

'What a strange contraption,' Mel said, peering down into the trench. 'It looks as though half a windmill has fallen in on its side.' The machine was a conglomeration of wooden planks, struts, and wheels, with hooks suspended from its various arms. In the centre, two wheels were attached to the middle core. Two men were straining hard, keeping these wheels constantly turning, allowing the arms with the hooks to travel up and down. Men on the floor of the canal attached full wheelbarrows to the suspended hooks, while others exchanged them for empty ones at the top.

'What a brilliant idea,' Mel said.

'Look, Rupert Johnson is standing over there. He certainly doesn't look too happy about it,' Hannah said.

'Not happy? He seems to be positively glowering,' Mel replied, giggling. 'You'd have thought he'd be pleased with the idea of speeding up the construction.'

'Maybe he's jealous.' Hannah suggested. 'It can't be much fun having other people brought in over you like that.'

'I don't know. I think there's something fishy about our resident engineer.'

Her aunt looked surprised. 'What d'you mean, Mel?'

Mel shook her head. 'I don't know really. It's nothing I can put my finger on—just a gut feeling.'

'Isn't that Josh's sister, Fleur, with him? They seem very pally. Does Josh know about this?' Hannah asked.

Mel shook her head. 'I don't know. I haven't liked to tell him. After all, she is my friend.'

'Well, if you won't, I will. I'm sure her parents wouldn't approve, taking into account her age and social standing,' her aunt said. 'Someone should stop her from making a fool of herself.'

Just then, their attention was drawn to an important-looking man striding up and down the edge.

'That's the inventor of this contraption, Edward Haskew.' One of the villagers told them. 'He's just been telling us that it can carry nearly one and a half thousand loaded barrows of soil from the bottom of the diggings up to a distance of forty feet in twelve hours.'

Both Mel and her aunt were amazed.

'And worked by just two men!' His neighbour added with awe.

Mel grinned at him. 'Plus all those filling and emptying the wheelbarrows,' she pointed out.

'Still, at this rate, the canal will be finished by Christmas,' her aunt added.

'Good job, too. I can't wait to see the back of this lot,' someone muttered. 'They've brought nothing but trouble.'

'It will be worth it when it's finished, you wait and see.' Mel couldn't resist defending her faith in canals. But many of the villagers shook their heads in disbelief.

'Come on, lass, I think now is a good time to head for home—before you start a riot,' her aunt told her with a laugh.

They made their way back across the fields arm in arm, enjoying the warm sunshine and savouring their few snatched minutes away from the chores of the farm.

The next morning, clouds were building up on the horizon.

'Reckon we'll have rain before the day's out,' John predicted during breakfast.

Mel sighed. 'Oh dear, I suppose that will be the end of all this lovely weather we've been having.'

'We need the rain, lass. The ground is as dry as a bone.' Her uncle pointed out.

'You farmers are all the same.' His wife teased. 'If it's fine, you want rain; if it's wet, you want it dry. You're never satisfied.'

'Well. That's the joy of farming,' John said with a shrug, and they all laughed.

The rain came just as they were getting ready for bed. It came with a vengeance, together with a terrific thunderstorm. Mel lay shivering under the bedclothes, too frightened to sleep. Would she ever conquer her fear of thunder? Eventually, the storm began to ease away. Mel was at last beginning to dose off when she became aware of a loud knocking. Wide awake once more, she sat up in bed. What was happening? The knocking came again, louder than ever. She heard her aunt and uncle moving about and a murmur of voices. Slipping out of bed, she pulled a shawl round her shoulders and ventured downstairs to find out what was going on. Was that Josh's voice she could hear? What was he doing here at this time of night? Something terrible must have occurred. She crept further downstairs, fearful of what she would find. But by the time she had made it to the bottom, Josh had disappeared outside.

'What's going on, Aunt Hannah?' she asked.

'It's Ben,' she sobbed.

Mel sighed. She presumed this meant Ben had been brought home drunk again. But when Josh and Connor came back in carrying Ben between them, she gasped in shock. Not only were his clothes soaking wet and muddy, but his face was a mass of blood and bruises. This was obviously something more serious than just getting drunk. Not one to allow sentiment to get in the way of practicalities, her aunt took a deep breath and opened the front room door.

'Take him straight in onto the truckle bed, boys, and remove his wet clothes. Carefully, mind, we don't yet know what other injuries he's suffered, poor lad. Quick Mel, run upstairs and fetch a pile of clean towels and sheets from the linen cupboard. I'll stoke up the fire and get some water boiling. John, find a couple of your clean shirts for these boys too, before they catch their death.'

Connor shook his head. 'Not for me, Mrs. P; I must be off as soon as we've settled Ben.'

'Well, thanks for bringing him home, Connor. You probably saved his life. I can't understand how he got into this state. Ben has never been one for fighting.'

'I gather he'd been mouthing off down the tavern all week about how he hated the navvies for attacking his wife and ruining his life,' he explained. 'I suspect one or two of them decided to get their own back. Though I doubt anyone will admit it. They made sure it happened out the back so there'd be no witnesses.'

Hannah shook her head, gazing sadly at her poor son. 'Perhaps in the future, he'll stay out of the tavern and pay more attention to Ruth.' Turning her attention back to the job at hand, Hannah soon had everyone organized into a flurry of activity. Her husband was told to fetch the warming stones from the washhouse to heat up in the fire, ready to be wrapped in flannel to warm Ben's bed. Mel delivered the towels only to be sent off immediately to fetch the herb salves and tinctures from the still room. Connor had already gone by the time she got back. Handing them over to her aunt, Mel was shocked at the sight of Ben lying there, battered and bruised and so deathly still. It frightened her.

'He's not dead, is he, Aunt Hannah?' she whispered uneasily.

'No dear, he's still alive. But he'll need a lot of care and the good will of God to keep him that way. Now you run off to bed, and leave us to cope here. Someone has to be bright and lively in the morning to get the work done.'

'I'll be off too, Mrs. Preston, if you don't need me anymore,' Josh said.

Hannah looked up from tending her son. 'Yes, of course, Josh. Thank you for helping Ben. It was good of you.'

'Not at all. I'll look in later in the week to see how he's getting on.'

Mel lingered, shivering in the hall, unable to face going back to bed. On his way out, Josh urged her to go up.

'You'd best get some sleep, Mel. They'll be relying on you in the morning to keep things running.'

'How can I sleep, not knowing if Ben will even survive?' she sobbed. He gathered her into his arms and held her close.

'Now, now, this won't do. I always took you to be the strong one. Crying won't help anyone. You won't be much help tomorrow if you're half asleep. So do as your aunt said, there's a good girl. You know she knows best. It certainly won't help anyone if you catch a cold, standing around in this freezing hall now, will it?'

She knew he was right, but it felt so safe in his arms. She didn't want to leave him. He lifted her chin with his finger and looked into her eyes. She thought—no, hoped—he was going to kiss her. But instead, he placed a swift kiss on her forehead and pushed her gently towards the stairs. With a sigh and a tearful smile, she did as he asked and slowly mounted the stairs to her little attic room. She could hear the rain still hammering on the windowsill, but thankfully the thunder seemed to have abated. Why, she wondered, did thunderstorms always seem to bring catastrophes into her life?

The following morning it was still raining hard, although the thunder was still absent. She found her aunt sitting beside Ben's bed.

'How is he, Aunt Hannah?'

'Still no change I'm afraid, Mel. I think you should run over to Ruth's after breakfast. It's time someone told her what has happened. Then we must hope she'll come here to be beside her husband.'

'Do you think she will? She hasn't left her house since the attack.'

'She must, otherwise I don't think he'll pull through.'

Mel ran all the way to the cottage. Thankfully the rain had eased off, though the hovering black clouds promised more to come. Mel found Ruth still scrubbing and polishing the already spotlessly clean cottage. She was just as abrupt and unwelcoming as before, but Mel tried hard to get through to her.

'Ben needs you, Ruth. He's been badly hurt and may not even pull through. You must go to him,' she pleaded. But Ruth merely shook her head and continued polishing. It was as though she had shut everything out of her mind except her perpetual cleaning. With a sigh, Mel was just about to admit defeat when she looked through the window and noticed the Reverent Crossly walking down the path. Surely if anyone could persuade Ruth, it would be her father. Mel met him on the doorstep.

'Morning, Reverend.'

'Morning, Mel. How is she this morning? Any change?'

'I'm afraid not, Reverend. I came to take her to the farm to be with Ben, but she won't come.'

'Is Ben drunk again then?' the Reverend asked sadly.

'No, he's been badly beaten up and Aunt Hannah is worried that he won't recover. She says Ruth needs to be with him. But she won't agree.'

'That's terrible. I'll see what I can do. I agree, she should be with him—marriage is all about being together through sickness as well as health.'

He went inside and Mel decided to leave them to it. Instead, she wandered round the little cottage's garden. The pigsty at the bottom was still empty. Someone had begun planting a few vegetables, but now it was looking sad and neglected. The little herb plot that Ruth had been so enthusiastic about, looked abandoned. Weeds were already encroaching on the young herb plants, choking them out. Mel felt the tears fill her eyes. Would that happy, loving Ruth ever reappear? Or would she permanently stay the hard, obsessive, uncaring person she had become? She hoped not. She missed the old Ruth so much. Oh, why did this have to happen? Despite having always been in favour of canals, Mel now wished this one had never been started. The cottage door opened and the vicar came out, leading a reluctant Ruth by the hand. Together they made their way to the farm. Hannah met them at the door.

'Thank goodness you've come,' she said, giving Ruth a big hug. Ruth just stood stiffly in her arms, but Hannah was undaunted. 'Come through and see Ben. He's still unconscious but I know he'll sense you're near.'

When Ruth saw her husband, she gave a cry. 'What happened? I thought he was drunk again. Oh, Hannah, he's not going to die, is he?'

Tears began streaming down her cheeks and she knelt beside the bed, taking Ben's limp hand in both of hers.

Hannah placed her hand on Ruth's shoulder. 'No dear, not if we can help it, but he's been badly beaten up and needs lots of very careful nursing if he's going to get better.'

Then Ruth broke down completely, sobbing loudly. Hannah gathered her into her arms.

'That's right, my dear,' she murmured quietly. 'You let it all out. It will do you good. I'm sure between us we'll get you both well again.'

Still standing in the doorway, Mel and the vicar were amazed at what they had just witnessed. The Reverend Crossly took Mel's arm.

'I think we should leave them to it,' he said. 'Let's go and make a warm drink.'

Mel nodded and led the way back into the kitchen. Mel bustled about warming some ale for them both, while Ruth's father sat in the wooden armchair deep in thought.

'I believe that's the first time Ruth has really cried since the attack,' he said. 'It will do her good to let it come out instead of keeping it bottled up inside her. I know it's tragic to see young Ben like that, but it could be the saving of them both. God moves in mysterious ways. It's obvious they still love each other. They've both got to admit it and work together to get over this.'

Later Hannah joined them.

'Ruth is calmer now, so I've left them together. I just hope I did the right thing bringing Ruth here. All we can do now is wait and see.'

'And we must pray,' the vicar added. 'I must be away now. Call me if you need me. No doubt I shall see you all at church on Sunday.'

'We'll be there.' Hannah handed him his hat. 'Now come along, Mel, there are a lot of chores to catch up on.'

As Mel went out to feed the chickens, she felt a shiver of apprehension. Would Ben really get better? Surely nothing else could go wrong, could it?

CHAPTER 17

When Mel arrived downstairs the next morning it was to find that Ben had taken a turn for the worse, having developed a raging fever. Her aunt and Ruth had spent the night alternately sponging his over-heated body with cold water and trying to keep a pile of blankets on him. They were both exhausted, and obviously very worried.

'He will get better, won't he, Aunt Hannah? Mel asked anxiously.

'Only God knows that. Now make yourself useful. I need some lavender, camomile, and valerian tincture from the still room. Quickly child, and then see to the breakfasts.'

As Mel hurried to do her aunt's bidding, she bumped into her uncle coming in from milking.

'Is my breakfast ready yet? I haven't got time to hang about.' He snapped.

'It won't be a minute, I need to get a tincture for Ben,' she told him.

'It should be ready by now, so get a move on. Then I shall need you to help feed the animals. Buttercup is due to calve and we could have trouble, her being so small.' He slipped off his boots and sat down.

Mel chewed at her lip. 'But I'm not good with animals, Uncle. You know that.' Just the thought of helping a cow calve made her feel sick.

'You've been with us long enough to get used to them, and with your aunt having to care for Ben, that only leaves you. So you have to do it. Now hurry up and stop whining.'

Tears filled her eyes. 'I'm not whining, it's just that the animals don't seem to like me,' she muttered to herself as she fled to the still room. Gathering up all the things on her aunt's list, she hurried back to the sick room, then turned her hand to getting breakfasts. Her mind was so fuzzy with worry that she even managed to burn that. Though in the end, only her uncle felt like eating any of it.

'There are the geese and pigs to let out and feed, the hens will need seeing to, and then you need to come to the cowshed in case I need your help with Buttercup,' he barked at her while pulling on his boots. Then he was gone.

'Run along,' her aunt said, hearing Mel's sigh. 'We're relying on you, dear. You know you can do it.'

Reluctantly, Mel tugged an old shawl around her shoulders and made her way towards the goose pen, picking up the bucket of corn on the way. The gander hissed his usual welcome.

'If you want your breakfast you'd better behave yourself,' she warned him, scattering the corn as she opened the pen. With a sigh of relief, he seemed more interested in the food than accosting her. She was just thinking that this was not so bad when her uncle shouted at her.

'The bucket of scraps for old Bertha is just inside the barn. Mind you, don't let her babies get out.'

At the sound of his voice, she turned towards him,

forgetting the golden rule of never turning your back on the gander. The vicious bird was quick to take advantage, giving her a hard peck on the calf of her leg.

'Ow, that hurt you brute,' she yelped, though the thickness of her skirts saved her from the worst of it. She swung the bucket at him, catching him by surprise and knocking him off his feet. 'Serves you right. I don't care if I've killed you,' she snapped, as she hurried off to collect the pig's food.

Bertha had recently given birth to ten little ginger piglets. They were scampering around their mother and everywhere. Normally Mel would have delighted at the sight. But today, whenever Mel tried to open the door of the pen, they kept wriggling through, trying to escape. She was fully occupied with pushing them back in, giving her no chance to get through herself. In the end, she decided to lean over the low wall and tip the scraps into the trough that way. But even that was not straightforward and the little ones kept getting into the trough. Bertha was getting more agitated with every aborted attempt and flung up her head, knocking the bucket from Mel's hand. It fell into the pen with a loud clatter, setting off the piglets squealing in fright. Mel shouted at her in frustration, bringing her uncle out of the milking shed to see what the commotion was about.

'What you are playing at, girl,' he shouted. 'Get in there and pick up that bucket.'

'No, I can't. I hate the animals,' she sobbed. With tears streaming down her face, she dashed into the barn and collapsed onto the hay, giving in to all the worries and fears that had been building up inside her. Suddenly she felt a hand on her shoulder and she tensed, waiting for a dressing down from her uncle. But instead, she heard Josh's voice gently reassuring her.

'It's alright, Mel, I've retrieved the bucket. Don't cry.'

When had he arrived? She hadn't heard him. She turned and collapsed into his comforting arms, feeling safe at last. He held her close, his hands gently massaging her back.

'Come now, Mel. It's not like you to give in like this. Where's that feisty fighter ready to take on the world? Show them you can do it.'

'I can't, Josh,' she hiccupped. 'It's too much. I feel I'm being sucked into a quagmire and I'm too tired to carry on.'

With one finger, he lifted her chin and looked into her eyes.

'You can do it. I know there's a streak of steel in there somewhere. You just have to believe in yourself. I know circumstances have been rather overwhelming lately, but it's nothing you can't get through. Remember, there's always a light at the end of the tunnel.'

He bent to kiss her forehead just as she tilted back her head and instead, it was their lips that met. The kiss was only light, gently brushing her mouth. But the sudden sensations that thrummed through her were startling. He must have felt it too, for they stared at each other in surprise. The tension was so tangible it was almost as though they could touch it. Unable to resist it, he kissed her again. This time deepening it into something meaningful, his mouth slanted across hers, lips parted, the heat of his mouth burning against hers, the pressure of it causing an odd tingling sensation low down in her belly. It felt so right. It was like coming home. Her fingers instinctively threaded through his hair, pulling him close, driving all rational thoughts from her mind. Nothing mattered beyond this moment. This was what she had yearned for, dreamt of, for so long. But even as Josh's hands caressed her trembling body, the sound of her uncle's shouts brought them crashing back to the real world.

'Mel, where are you? The hens haven't been fed yet. Then I need your help in the cowshed. Buttercup has started calving. Come on, there's no time for sulking. Get a move on.'

'Calving!' Mel gasped. 'Oh Josh, I can't do it. I'm a city girl.'

'Of course you can do it.' Josh gave her a little push. 'You've been a country girl for several months now and adapted very well. And John won't expect you to do anything you can't manage. Go to it, love; show them what you're made of.'

Scrabbling up off the hay, Mel brushed down her skirts, gave Josh a feeble smile, took a deep breath, and went off to see to the hens with Josh's smile warming her heart. If Josh believed in her, then she could do anything. While collecting the eggs, she was floating on a cloud. But meeting her aunt as she took them back to the farmhouse, she remembered Ben, and how his life was still hanging in the balance. She came back to earth with a bump. Life was far from perfect. She had no right to be feeling like she did—not when others were suffering. And what had happened to the vow she had made not to allow Josh to get too near? Taking the eggs back to the farmhouse, Mel saw her aunt coming out of Ben's room.

'How is Ben, Aunt Hannah? Is he going to be alright?'

'He's still burning up. We're trying to cool him down by sponging him with cold water. I'm just off to get some fresh.'

'Can I help? It seems unfair to leave it all to you and Ruth.'

'No, dear, Ruth is being a brick. I really believe it has done her good to realize Ben is suffering more than she is. And she does truly love him. That will help him fight this more than anything. You're helping most by doing our outside work. Your uncle is depending on you now.'

'But, Aunt Hannah, he wants me to help with calving. I can't do that. I know nothing about calving cows,' Mel protested.

Hannah gave a small laugh. 'Don't worry, dear. Your uncle

is not likely to risk the health of one of his precious cows by asking you to do anything drastic. He probably needs a hand keeping her still.'

Mel gave a sigh of relief and hurried over to the cowshed.

'At last,' he greeted her. He was standing at the rear of Buttercup, who was obviously well into the throes of calving. But the poor cow was very agitated, shifting around and throwing up her head. 'Can you grab her halter and try and calm her down? This is her first calf, so she's naturally anxious. I don't want to lose it – or her.'

Mel gingerly caught hold of the cow's head collar and tried to calm her down, patting her neck and talking softly to her. At first, she took no notice of Mel's efforts, but then she slowly calmed down, allowing John to help the calf arrive. It lay on the straw, all wet and helpless. John rubbed it with a handful of clean straw until it lifted its head, shaking it in bewilderment. Mel let go of Buttercup's halter and the cow turned to stare at the strange thing that had suddenly appeared in her stall.

Mel laughed and patted her neck.

'Yes, you've done it. That's your lovely little baby,' she told her. Buttercup went over and tentatively sniffed it. Then she began licking it dry. John patted the cow on her rump. The little calf immediately tried to stand, managing to get its back legs straightened. But when it tried to bring its front legs up as well, it wobbled and collapsed back down onto the straw. Mel couldn't help laughing. 'Come on, little one, you can do it,' she whispered. Then it tried again, this time successfully standing on all four legs. It promptly wobbled over to its Mum and started suckling.

John was well pleased. 'Well, done, old girl, you've got a healthy little heifer. And well done, Mel. She actually listened to you. I think you've got a real knack with animals.'

'Oh no, animals never like me,' Mel protested. 'They always go for me.'

'That's because they sense you're afraid of them. Animals are very sensitive to people's moods. You weren't afraid of Buttercup, were you?'

'Well, no, not when I realised how unhappy she was. I just felt sorry for her and wanted to help her.'

'Exactly, and once you accept the fact the animals don't want to hurt you, you'll get on fine. As I said, you've got the knack. Not everyone has, and I wouldn't have believed it of you if I hadn't witnessed it myself. You've hidden depths, girl. We'll make a proper country lass of you yet. Now, come on, let's leave mother and daughter to get acquainted while we go and get a drink. I think we deserve one.'

Mel felt exhilarated, as though a great weight had been lifted from her shoulders. Life was looking up. Now it just needed for Ben to get better.

The next morning Mel was greeted with the news that Ben had passed the crisis point and the fever had broken.

'Is he really on the mend, Aunt Hannah?' Mel was almost too nervous to ask.

'Yes, he's turned the corner and is sleeping. He just needs to get his strength back now. I've sent Ruth home to get some sleep herself.' Her aunt told her. 'The poor girl can hardly keep her eyes open. I'll be keeping a watch on Ben, so we shall still want you to help with the outside jobs I'm afraid.'

'That's alright. I'm getting more confident now since I helped Buttercup with her calf. But will Ruth be alright back at her cottage? You don't think she'll start her cleaning obsession again, do you?'

'I hope not, but we've got to risk it. Help her put things

into perspective. Now get some breakfast in you and then run along. I shall need some more herbal recipes made up soon.'

Mel's first stop outside was at the cowshed, to see how the little calf was getting on. She was thrilled to see it scampering round her mother, as bright as a sunbeam. Her uncle came over.

'You can name her if you like,' he told her. 'We usually use flower names.'

'I shall call her rosemary because that's a herb.'

John laughed. 'You and your herbs! I've never known anyone so taken with a subject as you.'

'Well, Rosemary is for remembrance, and I shall never forget my first calving.'

'Do you think you can manage the pigs today? Take a broom to push the little ones back. Look, I'm sorry I snapped at you yesterday, but it was a trying time.'

'It's alright, Uncle John. I think we were all overwrought. But thankfully Ben appears to be on the mend, and I'm getting used to things now.'

With a wave, John went back to his cows and Mel got on with feeding the other livestock. Then she headed for her herb garden. Running her fingers through the fragrant leaves, she felt a feeling of well-being engulf her. After the horror of the past days, things were finally looking good. Ben and Ruth were both on the mend, and Josh had kissed her. And oh, that kiss! Mel felt the thrilling tingles run through her just thinking about it. How she longed to repeat it, to enjoy it without being interrupted. Even as she reminded herself that he was out of bounds, she knew there was no way she would be able to resist him if he wanted to kiss her again. Maybe her father's crime wouldn't matter if they really loved each other? After all, Birmingham was a long way away. She sighed, knowing she would just have to wait and see how things panned out. Now she must get a move on, and replenish the supplies in the still room.

Much to Mel's disappointment, she didn't see Josh again that week. Her uncle had said he'd stopped by to enquire after Ben, but only momentarily. She reassured herself that he was bound to be at church on Sunday. Never had she looked forward so eagerly to attending a church service—it felt as though Sunday would never come.

But come it did. And even then, they were late getting there; at the last minute, Ruth had changed her mind about going, deciding to stay with Ben. Everyone was seated by the time they arrived. Mel could see Josh sitting with his family. But, as well as his parents and Fleur, there was another occupant in their pew—a beautiful young lady, dressed in the very latest fashion, and smiling intimately up at Josh. However, what hurt Mel most was the fact that, when she followed her aunt and uncle to their pew, Josh was so absorbed by his charming companion that he didn't even glance her way. Fleur sent her a smug smile. Mel felt as though a knife had plunged into her heart. If this was what it was like to be in love, she wished it had never happened.

At the end of the service, the Benchards were the first to leave. As Josh passed Mel's pew, it looked as though he would turn towards her, but then his lady companion took his arm and he gave all his attention to her, sparing not even a glance towards Mel. The vicar delayed her aunt at the door, making enquires after his daughter and Ben, so Mel slipped past, hoping to snatch a word with Josh. But it was Fleur that intercepted her.

'She's beautiful, isn't she?'

'Who?' Mel said, although she knew very well to whom Fleur was eluding.

'Carolyn Flemming-Smythe, of course—the lady Josh is going to marry. She's a real lady, not some trumped-up tradesman's orphan.' Mel winced. That hurt. To think she had once thought Fleur would be her friend. 'So you can forget any ideas you might have in that direction.'

'Oh but he—!' Quickly she shut her mouth. It was too late; she realized she'd given herself away.

Fleur laughed triumphantly. 'I knew it. He's made a pass at you, hasn't he? But you must realize that he didn't mean anything by it? Josh is gentry, and gentry are expected to sow a few wild oats with the lower classes before they settle down.'

Mel gasped. Was that what she was—wild oats?

'What about your own romance?' she asked, hitting back. 'The canal will soon be finished now they've brought in this new-fangled machine. Then the engineer will be moving on.'

'You're a bit behind the times. That machine wasn't man enough for the job. They've abandoned it and are back to doing it all by hand. Rupert won't be going anywhere for some time yet,' Fleur shot back before flaunting after her family and into their coach.

Mel was very quiet on the way back, and as soon as she could, she escaped to the solitude of her herb garden. Josh's betrayal hurt, but it also made her very angry. Wild oats indeed! Well, she was not going to be anyone's 'wild oats', so he could think again. She straightened her shoulders. If she was truthful, she'd always known he could never be hers. Now she'd been warned, she'd make sure he never got near her again. Hadn't Josh called her a feisty fighter? They'd see; from now on, she'd be strong and stand firm. He was welcome to his la-de-da lady. She didn't care. She spent the next hour vigorously weeding her herb plot.

CHAPTER 18

Several days later it was decided that Ben was well enough to be moved back to the cottage, with Ruth in complete charge of nursing him. In the farmhouse, things soon slipped back into the usual routine. Of Josh, there had been no sign. No doubt he was too wrapped up with his lady friend. Well, he was welcome to her, Mel told herself resentfully. Why should she care? It would be better if he stayed away completely. But it didn't stop her traitorous heart from longing for at least a glimpse of him. She couldn't get him out of her mind, her feelings for him were so mixed up. One minute she was filled with hate and resentment, determined to have nothing more to do with him. The next, she was remembering his kiss and longing for another. Just thinking of it, she felt a glowing excitement running through her body. If he ever tried to kiss her again she knew she would give in. Her thoughts were so full of Josh that she had difficulty concentrating on her work. Her aunt was getting very impatient with her. When she knocked over a full vat of cream she was supposed to be skimming, Hannah lost her temper.

'If you can't keep your mind on your job, you'd best get out of the dairy,' she shouted.

Mel went crimson with shame. Hannah never lost her temper. She must have really upset her. 'I'm sorry, Aunt Hannah. It won't happen again.'

'I'll make sure of that,' she was told. 'Here, take this butter and a few eggs over to Ruth. Perhaps the walk to the cottage will help clear your mind.'

Thankfully, Mel escaped. It was a lovely day and the skylarks were singing way up in the blue sky, which held only a scattering of white, fluffy clouds. Although thoughts of Josh were still pressing heavily on her mind, Mel's spirits couldn't help but respond to this sunny day. They lifted even higher when Ruth answered the door with a welcoming smile, reminiscent of the old Ruth.

'How's Ben?' Mel enquired. 'Judging from your smile, I guess he must still be on the mend. Aunt Hannah sent over some butter and eggs.'

'Yes, he's getting stronger every day. Come on in, it's good of you to bring these.' She took the proffered gifts. In the little kitchen, Mel was relieved to see that although everything was still spotless, a few things were lying around—so not as perfect as when she last visited.

'Ben's asleep at the minute and I'd rather not wake him. So if you're not in a hurry, perhaps we could have a drink first? I've just made a new jugful of elderflower cordial. It's very refreshing on a hot day like this.'

'That would be lovely, Ruth. But how are you now? It must all have been a terrible ordeal for you.'

'Yes, how I wish it had never happened. But as my father says, we must accept the trials the Lord presents us with, face them, and come out all the stronger for it.'

Mel couldn't help thinking that if the Lord was at all merciful, he wouldn't have let it happen in the first place, but she was sure that Ruth would believe her father knew best. And who was she to argue if it helped Ruth cope with it?

'Ben and I have now managed to talk about it, which has helped.' Ruth continued. 'You see, I felt so dirty after it that I couldn't imagine Ben ever wanting to touch me again. And then, when he tried to put his arms round me, I kept thinking how it felt when—you know—and I'd push him away. He'd tried to tell me he still loved me but I couldn't see how he could. So I shut myself off from everyone, even Ben. Ben coped with it in the only way he knew how—he tried to forget it all in drink. Well, you know what that led to.'

Mel merely nodded. It was obvious Ruth wanted to talk and she didn't want to interrupt the flow.

'But when I thought Ben was going to die,' Ruth continued, 'I realized how much my problems were affecting him. How selfish I had been, not seeing how he was hurting as well. I knew then that nothing mattered other than Ben's recovery. He is the only man I have ever loved, and I couldn't bear the thought of life without him.'

'I'm so glad he recovered and you are now putting it all behind you,' Mel told her.

'So am I. Although it's bound to take time, at least we're back on the right track. But what about you? It couldn't have been easy for you having to take over Ben's work.'

Mel laughed. 'The problem was, having been brought up in the city, I am still not completely comfortable around animals. Sometimes I was more of a hindrance than a help. Only this morning, I knocked over a full vat of cream I was supposed to be skimming, which was why Aunt Hannah sent me off on this errand.'

'I know we're all grateful for your help, Mel. I think you've done very well considering you've only been with us a short while. When you've been brought up in the country as we have, you tend to forget how frightening it must be at times. Do you miss the city?'

Mel shook her head. 'Not now. I did at first, but it wouldn't be the same there without my father. We were always together. He'd take me in to work with him right from when I was little. When I grew up, I even helped him with office work. I even imagined that if anything happened to him, I could continue running the business. But it was not to be.'

'Why not?'

'Because I'm a lady, and ladies aren't supposed to even want to do that sort of thing. It's a man's domain and woe betide any female that tries to trespass therein.'

Ruth put her arm round her. 'I'm so sorry, Mel.'

'I shouldn't complain. My aunt and uncle have been very good to me and I'm now beginning to love the countryside. Anyway, we can't always get what we want, can we?' Mel finished, her thoughts once more reverting to Josh.

'What you need is a steady boyfriend,' Ruth told her friend.

Mel laughed. 'Haven't you noticed, we're not exactly overflowing with candidates around here?'

'How about Josh? You both seem to get on well together.'

'Josh may treat the farm like his extended family but that doesn't mean he'd marry into it. Don't forget his father is a lord. He'll pick one of his own kind. In fact, I have it on good authority that he already has. She was in church with him last Sunday.'

'Did he tell you?'

'No, I didn't speak to him. He was too taken up with his girlfriend. She was very beautiful. But Fleur made a point of giving me all the details. I think she was warning me off. Not that I ever entertained any ideas in that direction.' *Especially with my past*, she added silently. Thankfully, this conversation was interrupted by a call from the bedroom.

'Ah, I think Ben must be awake. Would you like to have a word with him?' Ruth led her into the bedroom, where Ben was sitting up in bed. Mel was relieved to see how much better he looked.

'Hello Ben,' Mel greeted him. 'I see you'll soon be up and about and doing me out of a job.'

'When I get two lovely ladies visiting me in my bedroom, I'm tempted to linger here longer.'

'Oh no you don't, my lad.' Ruth scolded him. 'I've got more important things to do than run up and down stairs for you.'

Ben winked at Mel. 'See what a heartless wife I have to put up with,' he said, reaching out and patting Ruth's bottom.

Ruth blushed. 'Oh, you! Behave yourself. Whatever will Mel think of us?'

Mel just laughed. She was so glad that they had obviously overcome their problems and were well on the way back to normal.

'Anyway, Mel, I want to thank you for stepping into the breach after my stupidity. Can you forgive me?' Ben asked.

'Of course I can,' Mel assured him. 'Just promise to stay sober in the future. I can't wait to hand back my animal duties to you. I'm not sure that I will ever be completely at ease around animals.'

As they both assured her she would, she made her farewells and returned to the farm.

Talking about her past to Ruth had her thinking of her father's demise again. Had he really taken his own life? It seemed so out of character. He had always been full of new ideas he was going to try. She knew that the loss of his wife had hit him hard, but that had been years earlier. Even taking into account the blow he must have felt at the loss of his business, she would have thought he would have just turned around and put his mind to rebuilding it. Had he not thought of how it would affect her? Had she meant so little to him that he was prepared to leave her with nothing? Mel shook her head at her thoughts. It was so out of character, she just wouldn't have believed he'd do such a thing. But he had, and it had left her not only with nothing, but also with his terrible crime hanging over her head. No decent man would risk marrying her now. Certainly not Josh.

Oh, father, why did you just give up? You always drummed it into me never to give up when things didn't go the way you expected. She wouldn't have believed it if Rupert Johnson hadn't told her it was true.

Back at the farm, Mel headed for her herb garden, where she sought the calming peace that the scent of the herbs usually gave her. But today she found it difficult to stop her mind from swirling around the problem, and her feelings for her father and Josh. Thinking of Josh reminded her of their kiss. For a while, she allowed herself the weakness of savouring that special time when she had been in his arms and the magical moment of that kiss. Had it really meant nothing to him? Then the reality of her situation forced her to come back to earth. To face the brutal truth that Josh was not for her. She was so lost in her thoughts, that the sudden appearance of him striding purposely towards her startled her. She looked around frantically, but there was nowhere to hide.

'What do you want?' she asked abruptly.

Josh looked rather taken aback. 'That was not the welcome I was expecting. I thought the last time I was here we had parted on very friendly terms,' he said with a saucy twinkle in his eye.

'What occurred at our last meeting is best forgotten. It should never have happened,' she told him firmly.

Josh frowned. 'Why this sudden change of mind? At church last Sunday, I meant to talk to you but . . .'

'It's alright, Josh. I know why you didn't talk to me last Sunday. Fleur explained it to me.'

'Oh, that's good. I didn't want you to get the wrong end of the stick.'

'No, I understand the situation very well. That's why I say our last meeting must be forgotten. I have no wish to repeat it. In fact, I would prefer it if you didn't call on me again. Now, if you'll excuse me, I have a lot of work to do. With Ben still not able to do anything, we are all very busy.'

Mel turned and, leaving Josh standing there staring after her, walked quickly into the house. She had to get away before Josh could notice her tears welling up. She would not break down in front of him. She still had her pride. Pride that wouldn't allow her to be part of his wild oat-sowing, no matter how much her body craved to just take what little he offered. She slipped quickly into the still room before her aunt noticed her. Selecting her pestle and mortar, she tried to banish her pain and frustration by energetically pounding up the herbs she'd picked.

For the days following, Mel threw herself into a frenzy of work, doing everything she could to stop herself from dwelling on what might have been. It was only at night, when sleep evaded her that she found her thoughts continually returning to Josh. If only things had been different. There had been no sign of Josh since that day so he must have taken her at her word. She should be glad. But it hurt all the same. Would this pain ever lessen? They say time is a great healer. But how much time did it need?

Mel did her best to keep a cheerful face so that her aunt and uncle wouldn't start asking questions, but it wasn't easy. The weather didn't help either, as the long spell of sunshine had deteriorated into a steady drizzling rain. Also, the black clouds hovering on the horizon promised worse to come. As she continued her animal feeding duties, Mel seemed to be constantly wet and muddy. This was one aspect of farm life she felt she would never get used to. Staring out across the rain-soaked fields, she wondered how the canal navvies were faring. It must be worse for them with all that wet mud ev5ueywhere. Would this rain cause another fatal landslide like the one earlier that year? She hoped not. But when she spied Connor hurrying across the field towards them, she feared the worst.

'Is Rupert Johnson here?' he gasped as soon as he could catch his breath.

'I haven't seen him. What's happened? Is it another landslide?' Mel asked. Her uncle came hurrying over, sensing something wasn't right.

'What is it, lad,' he asked. 'Has someone been hurt?'

'No, but I must find the engineer immediately. The navvies haven't been paid and they are talking of forming protest riots. I must find him before things get out of hand.'

'I don't think he's here. But you'd better run up to his room, Mel, just to make sure.'

Mel sped off, wondering what would happen if he couldn't be found. She went to knock on the door but found it ajar. On entering she was astonished to find the room empty and no sign of any clothes or any other articles belonging to the engineer. Rupert Johnson had apparently packed up all his belongings and vanished. She rushed downstairs with the bad news.

'Oh, begorra, that's torn it. The lads are talking about

going into Gloucester and raiding the shops, demanding goods in lieu of money.' Connor sighed. 'There's bound to be fighting and even worse if we can't stop them.'

'Perhaps we can get Josh to talk to them?' John said. 'His father's one of the governors of the canal trust. Maybe he can talk them out of it? Speak of the devil—here he comes.' They looked up to see Josh driving his curricle towards them at full speed. Mel's heart thudded in her breast. What other terrible thing had occurred to make Josh spring his horses like that? Jumping down, he threw the reins over the gatepost and strode towards them.

'Where's Rupert Johnson?' he barked with no preamble

'That's what we'd all like to know,' Connor told him.

Mel frowned. 'He appears to have gone.'

'Gone where? Is he at the canal workings?' Josh turned towards his horse as if to make another mad dash to the canal. John put a hand on his arm.

'Slow down, Josh. I don't know what's up, but Connor here has just come from the workings because he's desperate to find him. However, he appears to have vanished.'

'What d'you mean – vanished?'

'Mel went up to his room, and it was empty. He's taken all his belongings and vanished,' John explained.

Josh groaned. 'Oh no. then it's true!'

'What is it, lad? What's happened?'

'I've just found this note from Fleur. She says she and Johnson are in love and because they know I'd never consent to the marriage, they are eloping. I'd hoped to catch them before things had gone too far, but it appears I'm too late. Did you know anything about this, Mel?' Josh demanded.

Mel flushed guiltily. 'I knew she'd been seeing him but I didn't think she'd do anything stupid. After all, he's a lot older than her. I thought the whole thing would fizzle out of its own accord.'

'And you didn't think to inform me of any of this?' Josh shouted at her.

'She was my friend. It didn't seem right to betray her confidences.' She stammered.

'You realize that by letting me know, you could have prevented your friend from making the biggest mistake of her life? I have to try and catch up with them. If any of this gets out, her reputation will be ruined.' Josh continued.

'I'm sorry, I thought . . .' Mel was going to explain that her aunt was going to tell him, but realized that with everything else going on, it must have slipped her mind. She stammered "I mean, I didn't think . . .'

'No, you didn't think. You were too busy worrying about yourself, weren't you?' Mel flinched at his accusations.

'They can't have got far. I must try and catch them up.' Josh continued. 'Do you know what vehicle he was driving?'

Mel shook her head. 'He hasn't got a vehicle.'

'Then he'd have to hire one in Gloucester. So I'll start there.'

'Wait, let me come with you.' Mel called as he turned away. 'If I am with her when we return, it will stop any rumours. We can say we were together all the time.'

Josh paused. 'That makes sense. Perhaps you can undo some of the damage you've done.'

Mel flinched again.

'Come on then. There's no time to waste. Where are you going now?' he asked as Mel dashed to the house.

'Just to get my shawl. Won't be a minute.' She grabbed up her bonnet and shawl, avoided her aunt's queries, and raced back outside. She'd leave Uncle John to explain things to her.

'The navvies haven't been paid and are talking of rioting, what can we do?' Connor asked Josh.

'Go up to the manor and ask my father to have a word, see if he can defuse the situation. I must go after Johnson,' Josh told Connor as Mel scrambled up into the curricle. Thankfully the rain had stopped, though it still looked threatening.

Then they were away, rattling down the road towards Gloucester as fast as the horses would go. Mel clung on tight to the sides and tried to keep calm. The fact that this was all her fault hung heavily on her shoulders. She just prayed they would find them before it was too late.

CHAPTER 19

'What about the navvies? Do you think it's safe to go into Gloucester?' Mel asked nervously.

Josh glanced at her with raised eyebrows. 'What are you talking about? Why shouldn't it be safe?'

'Connor says they are talking of rioting because they haven't been paid. That's why he was looking for Rupert Johnson.'

Josh groaned. 'You mean he wasn't content to just elope with my sister, he's taken the navvies wages as well?'

'It very much looks like it,' Mel told him sadly.

'The scoundrel; is there no end to his treachery? He must be caught.' He snapped his whip over the horses' heads, but they were going flat out anyway. As they hit a rut in the road, Mel gasped.

'At this rate, we shall be in the ditch,' she warned.

'Are you questioning my driving skills? I'll have you know I've raced against some of the finest Corinthians and won. In any case, speed is of the essence if we are going to catch the culprits,' Josh snapped at her.

After that, Mel didn't venture another word until they pulled into the Bell Inn's yard in Gloucester – thankfully still in one piece. Josh handed her the reins, telling her to keep them still, while he jumped down and disappeared into the inn. Mel looked nervously round the busy yard. Coaches and other vehicles rattled in and out over the cobbles, while ostlers bustled around, harnessing and unharnessing various horses. Shouted orders and enquires added to the continual noise. Mel prayed that her horses wouldn't take fright of anything; thankfully, they seemed to be glad of the rest. But then a big stagecoach rattled into the yard, coming very close to Mel. Her horses took fright and tried to rear. Mel screamed and jiggled the reins to try and get them to steady down. Where was Josh? Luckily, one of the ostlers grabbed the right-hand horse's head collar and, talking softly, managed to calm them down again. Mel felt weak with relief.

When Josh re-emerged from the inn, Mel was fuming.

'Don't you dare do that to me again,' she hissed, thrusting the reins at him.

He looked at her in astonishment. 'Why? What have I done now?'

'Leaving me in charge of these . . . these . . .'

'I thought you could manage them. I've given you a couple of lessons, and they were just standing still. What was so difficult about that?'

'Oh yes, they were standing still when you left,' Mel snapped. 'Until a great lumbering stagecoach nearly mowed them down. There was almost a terrible accident.'

'Everything seems alright now, so you must have managed,' he told her. 'But I will take note not to leave you in charge again, alright?'

Although thankful that she wouldn't be put in that situation again, she nevertheless felt piqued that he wasn't going to trust her anymore.

'Unfortunately, our quarry is still ahead of us,' Josh continued. 'He was here and had tried to hire a vehicle, but they hadn't got any available and sent him round to the livery stables off Hare Lane. So that's our next stop.' Climbing up next to Mel, he took the reins and expertly manoeuvred their way out of the crowded inn yard and onto Hare Lane. This time, when he jumped down, he tossed a coin to a tousled-headed youngster loitering nearby. The lad quickly snatched up the coin and, moving to the horses' heads, promised to mind them for him. Josh soon completed his enquiries and, tossing another coin to the lad holding the horses, jumped up and they were soon off again.

'Any luck,' Mel asked.

'Yes. The liveryman said a man fitting Johnson's description hired a covered brougham, but there was no girl with him.'

'So where do you think they're headed, Gretna Green or London?' She was surprised when Josh shook his head.

'Neither. Evidently, Johnson let slip that he was heading for Bristol.'

'Bristol?' Mel was astonished. 'I thought he was supposed to be eloping with Fleur.'

'I know, it doesn't make sense. To go to Bristol, he'd have to go back through our village.'

'As Fleur wasn't with him here in Gloucester, that must be where he was going to pick her up,' Mel pointed out. 'But why Bristol? It's the last place I expected them to go.'

'Maybe that's exactly why he picked it. But there's only one way to find out.'

With that, Josh turned the horses towards Southgate Street and the road to Bristol. As luck would have it, while passing through their village they saw the Rev. Crossley just turning into his gate, so Josh stopped and asked him if he'd seen anything of Fleur. The vicar confirmed that he'd caught a glimpse of someone earlier who looked like Fleur, being helped into a covered brougham which then took off at a cracking pace. Shouting his thanks over his shoulder, Josh was already whipping up his horses again in pursuit. Hoping they may have stopped on the way for refreshments, they called in briefly at the Berkley Arms and the Lion at Thornbury, but with no luck. So they pushed on into Bristol itself. Here, Josh turned the horses into the yard of the White Hart.

'I think it's best to leave the horses here and continue our enquires on foot,' he explained, helping Mel down. 'We'll grab some food here while we're at it. We can't afford to have you passing out for lack of sustenance, can we?'

'It's alright, I'm not hungry,' Mel protested, though her tummy gave a loud rumble lending a lie to her words. She blushed with embarrassment, but Josh merely laughed and ushered her in through the inn's dim entrance. The Innkeeper, recognising Josh as nobility, hastened to show them into a private dining room. Although small, the room was adequately furnished with a table and various wooden chairs. Also, a wooden settle with a high back, and a welcoming fire glowing cheerfully in a small, black-leaded grate. There was an aroma of beeswax and lavender mixed with the usual smells of beer and roast meats. Someone had obviously attempted to make it as pleasant as possible.

'I can offer you rabbit pie and mussels, just out of the oven, or there's a saddle of mutton,' the landlord said, rubbing his hands on the off-white apron that stretched around his rotund waistline.

'Just a platter of cold meats and cheeses will be fine. We are a bit pushed for time. And a tankard of your best ale. What would you like to drink, Mel, a little wine?' Josh asked.

Mel shook her head. 'A cup of chocolate would be lovely.'

'Certainly mam, sir, I will see to it at once.'

She suppressed a smile as the little man practically bowed himself backwards out of the door. Josh had obviously impressed the innkeeper. But she couldn't blame the man—when Josh put on what Mel called his 'Lord of the Manor' act, he could be very daunting. She was grateful that he wasn't like that all the time. A cheerful girl, whose ample figure looked in danger of spilling out of her servant's dress, brought in their drinks and covered the table with a selection of cold meats, pies and cheeses.

'Eat up,' Josh urged her. 'We haven't time to waste but you need to eat to keep your strength up.'

She didn't think she would be able to eat a thing because of her worry for Fleur, but the meat was deliciously tender and the cheeses so tasty that she soon put away a good plateful of the food. Josh did the same.

'Where do we go now?' Mel asked, once their plates were empty. 'Why would they come here? I thought they were eloping, so why didn't they head for Gretna Green?' So many unanswerable questions buzzed around in her head. None of this seemed to make sense. How could they find them when they didn't even know why they were here? She sighed.

'Don't look so down, Mel. We'll find them,' Josh assured her. 'Bristol is a busy port, so I'm guessing Johnson has arranged a passage on one of the ships that are berthed here. I'll make my way along the docks and see if I can pick up some clues. You'd best wait here. The docks are no place for you to be wandering around. There's a lot of rough people out there.'

'As I'm used to the canal navvies, they're not likely to shock me. Please let me come with you.'

But Josh was adamant, insisting she stayed in the inn until he returned.

Mel paced the room; the inactivity making the time drag. Where was Josh? Had he discovered Fleur yet? Had he discovered anything at all? Doing nothing was frustrating. She stared out of the window. Suddenly, she noticed a girl hurrying down the road, glancing around as though anxious no one would see her. Surely that was Fleur? Though the cloak and bonnet obscured her features, the bonnet looked familiar. Mel rushed outside and caught up with her as she was about to enter the stables.

'Fleur, wait, it's me, Mel,' she called, grabbing her arm. The girl pushed her away.

'Ere, wot d'you doing? Get yer 'ands arf me.' As she turned around, Mel could see she was nothing like Fleur.

'I'm sorry,' she stuttered. 'I thought you were someone I knew.'

The girl flounced away into the stables, leaving Mel feeling very foolish. She had been so certain it was Fleur. She could hear her talking to someone—no doubt relating how some silly girl had accosted her. Mel turned forlornly round to go back to the inn when she heard the person in the stables laugh. She froze, terror swamping her. She felt ill. She had never forgotten that evil laugh. It was imprinted in her mind. It was the laugh of the man who had assaulted her in the barn. The laugh of the man from the canal site who had attacked her and Ruth, and may have even killed other young women. Now that innocent girl was unknowingly going in to meet him. Did she know what he was like? She felt sick at the thought. Then, as she remembered what had happened to Ruth, she was overwhelmed with a terrible feeling of rage. That poor young girl; she couldn't let it happen. Without stopping to think, she rushed into the stables, shouting to her to get away from him. The girl took one look at her and fled out the back way. The man, waiting in the shadows, leapt out and grabbed her arm.

'What's got into you, yelling like that, upsetting my girl? You jealous or summut?'

Mel struggled, yelling

'Let me go,' but she couldn't get free of him.

'Not so hasty. I was looking forward to sampling her, but never mind, you'll do instead.' He laughed. That awful evil laugh that had filled Mel's nightmares for months. She struggled frantically but he merely laughed again. 'I like them with a bit of spirit. It makes things more interesting.' Mel was terrified. How she wished she'd stayed in the inn as Josh had told her. Now her impetuousness was to be her downfall. He pulled her against him, his mouth descending on her, making her want to gag. Instinctively, she bit down hard on his lip. He yelled and jumped away, pulling her head back by her hair. The pain brought tears to her eyes.

'You'll regret that, you bitch,' he hissed, tugging harder at her hair so that her head was bent right back.

'I know you,' he said, staring at her. 'You're that interfering bitch from the farm that cost me my job on the canal.' He pushed his face nearer hers. The smell of stale ale and sour breath nearly made her vomit. 'I had a cushy little number going there, doing odd jobs for that two-faced engineer. Then your interfering made things a bit too hot for me. But luck was still with me. Old Johnson needed a driver to take him and his bit of skirt to Bristol, so I seized my chance, didn't I? And look what lady luck has delivered into my arms. I shall enjoy extracting my revenge.' Mel struggled harder, kicking out with her feet, but he merely laughed and pulled her hair harder. She couldn't get free; he was too strong for her. Where was Josh? If only she'd stayed in the inn as he'd told her. If only she'd left a note. So many ifs. But it was too late now. She couldn't rely on him rescuing her. He wouldn't have any idea where she was or why she'd gone off. She brought the heel of her boot back hard against his shin, but he merely cursed and pulled so hard on her hair that she was sure he'd pull some out. She became dizzy. Just as she thought she'd pass out with the pain, two horsemen rode into the stables and shouted for assistance with unharnessing their steeds.

'What are you waiting for, man? Jump to it, unless you want my whip round your backside.' Her captive cursed again and bundled her out the back way. It opened directly onto the wharf, with a slipway allowing easy loading of the boats. Mel flung herself away from him, screaming as a handful of hair was left in his clenched fist. Then she rolled down the slipway. With a bellow of rage, the man lunged at her, slipped on the greasy cobbles, and tumbled over the edge into the water. There were shouts of 'man overboard', and people running, trying to pull him out of the water. Mel managed to crawl behind a barrel where she hid, trembling so much that she couldn't move. More shouts and she heard someone say:

'He's a goner. Never stood a chance. The Rose ploughed straight into him as she came into berth. There was nothing he could do. I wonder who he was.'

'Some drifter, I expect,' another answered. 'We get a lot through here. But wasn't there some wench with him?'

'Never saw one. There's no one around now. Come on, I need a beer after all that excitement.'

To Mel's relief, she heard the men move away, still talking over the incident. She stayed huddled behind the barrels, unable to find the strength to move, hardly aware of the sounds and voices milling around her. Eventually, she realized that she was cold and wet, and it was time she moved. Cautiously, she peered round the barrel. Although people were milling around, no one seemed to be looking her way, so she stood up and moved out into the crowd. But which way to go? The inn that she'd left didn't face this way and she just couldn't bring herself to go back through those stables. She walked aimlessly down the dockside. Oh, where was Josh? Suddenly she recognised a familiar face in the crowd. The relief was so intense that without another thought, she rushed up to him. Rupert Johnson turned as she clutched at his sleeve, his look of annoyance changing to a frown.

'Mel Meredith, what are you doing here?'

Her heart plummeted when she realized what she'd done. 'Oh, Mr. Johnson, I'm looking for . . . Um . . .' Would it be wise to let him know Josh was in the vicinity? 'Fleur,' she blurted out.

'What makes you think she's here?' he demanded. Then, suddenly he changed his tactics. 'You want to see Fleur, do you? Then I'll take you to her. Come along.' Although very nervous at this apparent capitulation, she allowed herself to be ushered along and onto a ship berthed alongside. Mel stopped.

'I don't think . . .' She began.

'It's too late to think.' He interrupted. 'You wanted to see Fleur, well, that's where I'm taking you. Now get down those stairs.' Opening one of the cabin doors, he pushed her in, slamming it shut. She heard the key turn in the lock. The cabin she was in wasn't very large, with narrow beds on each side. A small cupboard stood at the far end, below a dirty porthole. Fleur was sitting on one of the beds. But she looked very different from the sunny, glowing girl who had told Mel of her love for the engineer. This girl was pale and wan, with tears sliding silently down her cheeks. At the sight of Mel, she jumped up and flung her arms around her.

'Mel, oh I'm so glad to see you. But what are you doing here? You're trembling, and you're so cold?' Sitting her down on the bed, she wrapped one of the blankets around her, her own woes temporarily forgotten. For a while they just sat together, finding comfort in each other's arms. As soon as Mel had stopped shaking and she could think straight again, she asked Fleur what had happened to her.

'Has he hurt you?' she asked.

Fleur shook her head. 'Not physically. Oh, Mel, everything's gone wrong.' She was really crying now. 'It was so romantic. He treated me as an equal when everyone else still thinks I'm a child.' Mel could understand how that must have flattered her. It was not an easy age to deal with. 'I believed he genuinely loved me. When he asked me to come away with him, I thought we were going to Gretna Green to be married. Then we'd come back and my parents would have to accept him as my husband.'

Mel sighed. Fleur may want to be treated as an adult, but she was still living in a child's dream world.

'So why did he bring you to Bristol?'

'It wasn't until we were on the road that he told me we couldn't go back because he'd left his canal job, and we were going to France to start a new life together. But when I said I didn't want to go to France—I'd heard Josh talking about a lot of unrest over there—he just laughed and said it was a bit late to worry about that. But Mel, I do worry about it. I don't want to go to France. I may never see my family again. Why can't we go back?'

'I'm afraid he never had any intention of going back, because your knight in shining armour is a thief. When he left, he took all the navvies' wages with him. They are threatening to riot through Gloucester, ransacking the shops for the goods they can no longer buy.'

'Oh Mel, it's all my fault! If only I'd listened to you. What can we do?'

'First, we need to get back on shore.' But even as she got up to try the door, she felt the ship move. She groaned. 'I think it's too late, Fleur. I think we are already on our way to France.'

CHAPTER 20

Fleur promptly dissolved into a fresh bout of tears. Holding her close, Mel wracked her brain as she tried to think of a way out of this situation. But no matter how she tried, she couldn't think of any. If only Josh was with them. Where was he? Did he even know they were on board a ship? A ship bound for France! Mel felt like bursting into tears herself but knew she mustn't give in, for Fleur's sake. Her friend was obviously too distraught to think clearly. Hearing the key turn in the lock, she looked up in trepidation. Who was it? Friend or foe? However, the face that appeared at the door was no one they knew. At least it looked a friendly face—round, weather-beaten, complete with bushy grey brows and deep wrinkles that reminded Mel of the gnomes she'd read about in fairy tales. Even better, this gnome came bearing gifts. A flagon of weak ale and a platter holding a hunk of bread and a slab of cheese.

'I reckoned you young ladies might be hungry.' He told them.

'Thank you, sir,' Mel said, taking it from him.

'No need to 'Sir' me, me dears. I'm just an ordinary seaman. Just call me Jake. I've brought you a bite to eat. I've got two young 'uns like you at home, an' I know they're always hungry. But I should eat it up now, while we're still in the river. Once we reach the sea it could get a bit choppy.'

'Oh dear.' Mel bit her lip. 'Is it likely to be very rough? I've never been on the sea before.'

Jake nodded. ''Fraid so. Also, we could be in for quite a storm. I told the skipper it might be better to postpone sailing, but the nob that was with him insisted we set sail immediately. Don't you worry none, though. We're bound to come through alright. It will just be rather rocky, that's all. But mustn't linger. 'Ave my duties to see to.'

'Thank you again, Jake, for your kindness.'

He merely winked at her and left. Though this time Mel didn't hear the key turn in the lock, so that was a blessing. Turning to Fleur, she poured some ale into a mug and offered it to her.

'Come on, dear, take a sip. Then eat some of this bread and cheese, you'll feel better then.'

'I don't feel like it, Mel.' Fleur lifted her tear-stained face and grabbed Mel's arm. 'What are we going to do?'

Mel gently stroked Fleur's hair. 'There's nothing we can do at the moment except keep our strength up to be ready for the time when we can do something. So just eat up while we've got the chance.'

With a sigh, Fleur dashed the tears away with the back of her hand and grudgingly picked up a chunk of bread. However, after the first bite, she tucked into the rest with such gusto that Mel wondered when her last meal had been. Mel helped herself to a little of the ale but, as she had eaten earlier, left all the food for Fleur. When she'd finished, Fleur seemed a lot calmer, so Mel gently coaxed her to talk about their situation.

'I don't understand why you've been locked in a cabin like this. I understood that the two of you were very much in love.

But this is no way to treat a loved one. What happened to change everything?'

'It was when we came on board this ship. He took me down to this cabin that had just one huge bed in it. When I asked him where I was to sleep, he said there—with him. He was boasting about how we'd have the whole voyage to get to know each other. He was . . . sort of . . . well . . . leering. It frightened me.' Fleur began to cry again, but Mel helped her dry her eyes with her hanky and pressed her to continue. 'I told him that I couldn't possibly sleep with him before a priest had married us. It would be a sin, and I had no intention of condemning my soul to certain hell.'

Mel remembered how she'd felt when Josh kissed her. In Fleur's situation, she wasn't sure that she would have been able to resist. Maybe Fleur's heart wasn't as engaged as she thought. Suddenly she felt years older than Fleur, even though they were of a similar age. Dragging her thoughts back to the present, she listened to the rest of her friend's story.

'Then he went mad and started shouting at me,' Fleur continued. 'He said some terrible things and called me all sorts of names. Oh, Mel, I was terrified. I thought he was going to kill me. I'd never imagined he'd behave like that. I thought he was a gentleman. Oh, I've been such a fool to be taken in like this.'

Mel put her arm around her friend's shoulders. 'Don't feel too bad about it, Fleur. You weren't the only person he fooled. We all thought he was a gentleman. Do you think my aunt and uncle would have agreed to him lodging with them if they'd believed otherwise?'

'But you never liked him.'

'No, but I didn't believe he'd behave this badly. Oh, if only I could let Josh where we are,' Mel said. 'I know he was on the waterfront, but I don't suppose he knows which ship we are on.'

'Did Josh follow us?' Fleur burst into a fresh bout of tears. 'Oh, Mel, he'll be so cross with me,' she wailed.

'I'm sure he'd just be glad to have you back.' Mel shook her head sadly. 'Unfortunately, that is not looking very likely.' She felt like bursting into tears herself. What did Rupert Johnson have in store for them both? Mel felt sick with worry. Then she straightened her shoulders. She mustn't give in, for Fleur's sake. 'Come on now—dry those tears, love. While there's life, there's hope, as Aunt Hannah is always saying.'

But her words were drowned out by the creaking of the timbers as the ship keeled sharply, sending them sliding across the cabin. The girls grabbed each other as a loud rumble of thunder made the ship vibrate. Mel trembled, feeling a scream building inside her. But Fleur needed her to be strong. With a tremendous effort, she pushed down her own fears and concentrated on her friend. They could feel the waves buffeting the ship's sides. If only Josh was with them. She was cross with herself for not at least leaving a note. Now it was too late.

'Oh Mel, we're going to be drowned.'

Fleur's words were cut short as the ship keeled violently over to the other side, sending them tumbling back across the room. Mel felt an icy chill travel down her back. Was this to be the end of them? She had a fleeting moment of regret that she'd never known the ecstasy that Josh's kiss had promised. The turbulence increased alarmingly, together with creaks and groans from the surrounding woodwork. A ferocious storm must have sprung up very suddenly. The girls clung to each other, wedged in a corner to try and prevent themselves from being hurled around the cabin. The turmoil seemed to go on for hours. Poor Fleur turned green and was soon retching over the chamber pot. All Mel could do was hold her, murmuring words of comfort and reassurance. But she really needed reassurance herself. Was there no one to help them?

Oh, Josh–if only I'd stayed at the inn as you'd wanted. But even as the thoughts entered her head, she realized that if she had, Fleur would be facing this alone. Maybe this was destined to happen. Listening to the constant creaking and groaning of the ship's timbers she couldn't help but fear the worst. How much longer could they stay afloat? What would drowning feel like? Maybe it would just be like falling asleep. She hoped so.

Just as she had decided that there was no hope, the cabin door flew open and Jake was urging them to follow him, explaining that the captain had ordered everyone up on deck. They staggered along the corridor, trying desperately to keep their feet as the ship continued to throw them from side to side. With the help of Jake, they made it up the narrow stairway and out onto the deck. Up there, an angry wind whipped at their skirts and rain stung their faces. All around them was chaos. The top of the main mast had snapped off and hung in a tangle of ropes and torn sails. The ship was listing helplessly, moving closer to some vicious-looking rocks. Longboats were being launched. Time was obviously at a premium.

'Quickly, into the boat,' a familiar voice urged them. The girls' fear was tempered with relief as they recognised him.

'Josh! How did you get here?' Fleur gasped.

'I'd traced Johnson to this ship. I managed to slip aboard just as it was leaving. But Mel, you're supposed to be safe back at the tavern.'

'No time for a chat—get aboard, before it's too late,' Jake barked. Josh picked up Fleur and stepped into the boat as the men slipped it over into the water.

'Mel, jump in, quick,' Josh shouted.

Just then, another fork of lightning lit up the sky, followed closely by a loud, long rumble of thunder. Mel froze, her hands clasping the ship's rail so tight that they turned white. She couldn't move. Her old fear of thunder held her paralyzed. The boats had slipped away before anyone had realised. Even as the last longboat hit the water, she could see Josh shouting and waving his arms, but still, she stayed motionless. She squeezed her eyes shut. She had always known a thunderstorm would one day be the death of her. As another flash of lightning lit up the angry waves and those black jagged rocks grew ever nearer, she knew her time had come. An extra strong gust of wind buffeted her, nearly dragging her grip free from the rail. She opened her eyes and looked towards the longboat. It was being tossed about like a cork in fermenting whey. Josh was still shouting but the wind flung his words into oblivion. Then she saw him dive from the boat into the water.

'NO!' This wasn't supposed to happen. What was Josh doing? He mustn't die. She needed to get to him. Suddenly released from her paralyzing fear, she threw herself over the rail, plunging into the murky, roiling depths of the freezing sea. She had to get to him.

The water stung even through her clothes. Huge rolling waves engulfed her, dragging her down. But the image of Josh also struggling in the waves forced her to kick her legs, desperately clawing to reach the surface. Then Josh was there, his arms around her, and together they broke the surface with Mel gasping for breath. The men had manoeuvred the longboat nearer and were soon hauling them both up into its relative safety. Panting, they collapsed in a tangled heap at the bottom of the boat. Mel flung her arms around Josh's neck and hugged him so close that she could feel his heart pounding in rhythm with her own.

'I've got you. You're safe now,' he told her, even though the buffeting waves seemed to contradict him. She sat back. One of the seamen put his jacket around her shoulders as she was still shaking with cold and fear. She could feel the chill from the water right down to her bones, emphasizing the cold, but at least she was alive. And so were Josh and Fleur. The men turned their attention to rowing the boat towards the shore, Josh taking his turn at the oars. Mel shuffled along the boat to Fleur, who was looking very blue around the lips. Unable to speak, the two girls hugged each other. As the thunder continued to rumble overhead, the rain was sheeting down, making it very uncomfortable for them, crouched in the bottom, heads bowed, unable to see if land was near. Just when she thought the nightmare would never end, she felt the prow crunch onto sand and the welcome shouts of the locals who had come to help them all ashore.

'Are we in France?' Fleur asked tentatively as Josh helped the girls out.

'No, my dear. Luckily the wind was blowing towards England and we've finished up at a small fishing village off the south coast,' Josh told her. 'Now let's find you somewhere dry before you both catch a chill.'

A tubby little man with red cheeks and a woolly scarf came up to them.

'The men are being taken to the church hall, but you and the young ladies would be welcome to take shelter in my tavern, the Lobster Pot, sir. The name's Dodds. You'll find a good fire there to warm you, and I'm sure my good wife would be able to find some dry clothes for the ladies.'

'That's very good of you. Come along you two, the sooner we have you warmed up the better,'

The girls needed no further bidding, and they gratefully

followed their host along the quay to a long, low stone building whose candle-lit windows were half hidden under the jutting thatched roof. The dimly lit interior smelt of stale beer, cabbage water, and wood smoke. But the roaring wood fire in the inglenook fireplace drew the girls like moths to a flame. In complete contrast to her husband, the innkeeper's wife was as thin as a broom handle, her black hair scraped back in a tight bun. Mel thought she would look quite frightening except for the unexpected mischievous twinkle in her blue eyes, and her welcoming smile.

'Oh you poor dears,' she said. 'Come upstairs and let's get you out of those wet clothes. By then I'll have a nourishing bowl of vegetable stew ready for you.'

It was a relief to be out of their sodden garments and, wearing the couple's spare nightshirts and wrapped in blankets, they hurried back down to the fire. Josh had also shed his wet clothes and the girls couldn't smother their giggles at the sight of him in what was obviously their host's trousers. They barely reached his calves and were held up with twine. He grinned back.

'At least they're dry,' he said, pulling another blanket round his bare shoulders.

Mrs. Dodds bustled in with bowls of hot, fragrant-smelling stew and a platter of flatbread, saying, 'I'm sure you'll all feel much better once you've got this lot down you,'

The food certainly was delicious, but the girls were nearly asleep before they'd finished. So the good woman ushered them upstairs and tucked them both into the Dodds' own bed. Luckily, they were so exhausted that they slept soundly all night. The following morning, dressed once more in their own dried clothes, they all tucked into a hearty breakfast of fat bacon, eggs, and potato fritters. Josh had already been out and brought them up to date with the details.

'I'm sure you'll be relieved to know that everyone on the ship made it safely to shore and is accounted for, with one exception – Rupert Johnson. He is now nowhere to be found, and there seems to be some confusion as to whether or not he actually boarded a longboat. So at this time, we don't know if he perished when the ship broke up on the rocks, or if he slipped away unnoticed on land. Even if that is the case, I'm sure he won't show his face anywhere around Gloucestershire—you've nothing to worry about on that score.'

Fleur gave a sigh of relief.

'What about the money he stole?' Mel asked.

'Well, it could be at the bottom of the sea or disappeared somewhere with Johnson. Either way, I'm afraid we can say goodbye to ever seeing it again.'

Mel frowned. 'But what about the navvies' wages? And the canal—will they be able to finish it?'

Josh shook his head.

'Without any money or an engineer, I think they'll have no option but to abandon it—for now, anyway. Possibly, if they can raise enough money in the future, it may still get finished. The navvies will move on to other sites. I'm sure they'll find other work. At least the local villages can settle back into a peaceful existence again.'

'I shall be glad of that. The canal has caused too many problems for my liking.' Then Mel turned to her friend. 'But how do you feel, Fleur? It must be hard for you.'

'I'm so ashamed. How could I have been taken in by such a horrid man? I'm so sorry Josh, for causing you so much worry. And you, Mel–you've been a brick. To think I really believed he loved me. I shall never trust another man,' Fleur moaned.

Mel hugged her friend while Josh reassured her that they were just glad she was safe and that nothing too drastic had happened. Mel thought of Ruth and what had happened to her. She was so glad they had rescued Fleur before it had gotten to that stage.

'Never is a long time,' Josh teased. 'I'm sure if we can arrange a season in London for you next year, you will meet someone who will win your trust.'

Josh's words instantly brought the sparkle back into her eyes. 'Oh Josh, that would be wonderful. But how, Mamma isn't up to chaperoning me.'

Josh laughed. 'Don't worry, I'm sure we'll find someone to bring you out. Maybe our aunt in Bath might agree. And I could come up to London with you.'

'Oh yes,' she said, bubbling over with excitement. The horrors of the last few hours already forgotten in the resilience of youth. 'You can stand up with me at the balls. That way I shall be guaranteed at least one partner.'

'Now what have I let myself in for,' Josh groaned good-heartedly, glad there appeared to be no lasting effects from her ill-judged romance. 'Now, I must go and see if I can arrange some form of transport to get us home.' He looked to where Fleur was now chatting happily with Mrs Dobbs, then looked at Mel. 'Would you like to walk with me a bit, Mel?' he asked.

Mel and Josh walked down to the beach in silence. The rain had stopped but the wind was still whipping the waves up in a frenzy.

'It seems a miracle that we got out of that alive,' Mel said with a shudder.

Josh put his arm around her. 'I'm more than thankful that we did.' He told her. 'When I saw you still standing on that ship that was about to break up on the rocks, Mel, I felt a pain in my chest that took my breath away. I knew then that my life wouldn't be worth living without you. I shouted and shouted but you took no notice. I knew I had to somehow get to you.'

'Oh Josh, I didn't hear you shouting. The thunder was echoing round and round in my head. I couldn't move. All my life I have been petrified of thunderstorms. My mother died during a thunderstorm. I prayed and prayed to God to save her, but he couldn't hear me above the thunder. I've always believed that one day a thunderstorm would take me too. But not you. When I saw you jump into the water, I couldn't let it take you as well. So without thinking, I just jumped in as well.'

Tears were streaming down her cheeks

'Thank goodness you did. Oh my darling Mel, I couldn't bear to lose you.' He took her in his arms and kissed her. The kiss started as just a soft brush of her lips, but neither of them could resist deepening it until the thrill of it had them straining closer, eager for more, until some woman tapped them on the shoulder with her walking cane.

'Young man, we don't stand for that sort of behaviour around here,' she demanded, looking down her rather prominent nose at them. 'Stop it this minute.'

They broke apart, and Mel felt herself going very red. Josh muttered an apology and hustled her back to the inn. But before they entered, Josh stopped her.

'Before we join the others, I must ask—will you marry me, Mel?'

She pulled away from him. 'Oh Josh, I can't, I'm sorry.'

'But I thought . . . You don't care for me?'

'I do, very much! That's why I can't marry you. You see, my father committed suicide. He was a criminal. I can't let you sully your name by marrying me,' she sobbed.

Josh pulled her back into his arms.

'Oh, you poor girl. I don't care about your father or what he may or may not have done. It's you I love and it's you I want to marry, not your father. So, any more excuses for not marrying me?' he asked, lifting her chin and dropping a kiss on the tip of her nose.

'Oh Josh, I love you so much and I'd be honoured to marry you.'

'Good, then let's collect Fleur and go home.'

EPILOGUE

Three months later.

As Mel looked down into the deserted crater of the abandoned canal, she sighed. Josh tucked his wife's hand through his arm.

'What was that big sigh for, Mel?' he asked.

'It's strange, being so quiet after all the noise and bustle that used to fill it. Not a sound to be heard.' Just then, a cheeky robin flew down onto a broken barrow and began to sing, filling the air with its song. Mel laughed. 'Trust you to prove me wrong,' she told him. Then her frowns returned. 'It seems such a shame to see it like this after all the hard work the navvies put in. Do you think it will ever be finished?'

'Oh yes, I'm certain it will be one day,' Josh assured her. 'When they've managed to raise enough money and found a new engineer. This canal is too important to the trade in Gloucester for it not to be finished. At the minute, they're losing business because the ships negotiating the river Severn have to wait for the tide and then navigate shifting sandbanks. Though I'm not sure when that will be—possibly not until this war with France has ended.'

'Well, when they do finish it, let's hope it doesn't bring as many problems as last time.'

'But enough of wool-gathering. If we're going to call in on your aunt before our journey to London, we must get a move on,' Josh reminded her before handing her back up into the gig.

Mel turned her thoughts away from the canal and pondered on the future. She was in two minds about this trip to London. Yes, she was looking forward to seeing Fleur again, where she was preparing for her 'season' under the care of her aunt from Bath. She had already written, exclaiming excitedly over the fashions and sights she'd seen. But Mel was not so sure she'd like London. How would she fit in with Josh's crowd? Would they snub her because her father was in trade? She chewed worriedly at her lip.

'What's worrying that pretty little head of yours now?' Josh asked.

She smiled at him, banishing her morbid thoughts. They had no place on this lovely sunny day. She quickly reassured him that all was well, and shuffled along the seat so that she could feel her husband's body touching hers.

At the farm, Mel was pleased to find not only her Aunt Hannah and Uncle John, but also Ben and Ruth as well. There were welcoming hugs and kisses all round.

'You're just in time to join in our celebrations. Hannah is about to open a bottle of her special elderberry wine,' John announced, filling two more glasses.

'I'm always happy to sample your elderberry wine, Hannah, but what's the celebration? Josh asked.

John slapped his son on his back. 'Go on, tell 'em, son.'

With a big grin and a fond look at his wife, Ben lifted his glass and announced, 'Ruth and I are expecting our first baby.'

After adding their congratulations, Josh teased, 'First? You hoping for more?'

'We're hoping for a large family, God willing,' Ruth blushingly admitted.

Mel gave her friend a big hug. 'I'm so glad things have turned out right for you, both.'

'But what of you two?' Hannah asked. 'I must admit, married life looks as though it suits you. You're positively glowing.'

It was Mel's turn to blush.

'It's perfect, Aunt Hannah. Josh has had one wing of the manor converted for our own use, but we are still close enough to keep an eye on his parents.'

Hannah turned to Josh. 'How is Lady Benchard? I thought she look rather frail the last time I saw her in church.'

'Her health isn't too good now, I'm afraid.' Josh told them. 'But Pa still keeps going, having recovered over the upset about the canal.'

'Talking of the canal, have you heard anything of Connor O'Flynn?' Mel couldn't resist asking. She'd often wondered how the cheeky Irishman with the twinkling eyes had fared.

John nodded. 'He called in just before he left. He's decided to return to his father's farm in Ireland where, with the money he saved working the canal, he intends to start breeding racehorses.'

'I wish him the best of luck,' Josh said 'He wasn't a bad sort.'

Mel looked at him with raised eyebrows, remembering the time when he had referred to Connor as 'Scum', but she held her peace, changing the subject instead. 'I heard a rumour, Ruth, that your father has been seeing a lot of Widow Hunt lately? Do you think anything will come of it?'

'Time will tell,' Ruth laughed, 'Dad never was one to rush into things.'

'We must be off, I'm afraid,' Josh said, refusing John's offer of another glass of wine. 'We hope to make a reasonable distance towards London before stopping for the night.'

'We shall be residing in London for Fleur's season,' Mel added.

'And give my wife a season as well, as she never had the chance before,' Josh added, smiling fondly at Mel.

'You want to watch out, Josh. Some city Beau may turn her head,' John teased.

Mel smiled up at her husband. 'No chance of that, Uncle John. There's only one man for me.'

'Well, take care, both of you,' Hannah said, hugging them. Then, after many more hugs and handshakes, they were on their way.

Trotting away from the farm, Mel looked around with pleasure at the peaceful rural scene.

'It seems incredible to think I was once scared of all this. Now I love it.'

Josh grinned at her. 'I'd say you've adapted reasonably well for a city girl,' he teased.

She pulled a face at her husband. 'Mr. Benchard, I'll have you know I consider myself a fully-fledged country girl now.'

'Mrs. Benchard, I completely agree,' Josh laughed, 'and a perfect wife to boot.'

Printed in Great Britain
by Amazon

50232661R00128